ISBN 978-1-330-13631-7
PIBN 10034697

This book is a reproduction of an important historical work. Forgotten Books uses
state-of-the-art technology to digitally reconstruct the work, preserving the original format
whilst repairing imperfections present in the aged copy. In rare cases, an imperfection in
the original, such as a blemish or missing page, may be replicated in our edition. We do,
however, repair the vast majority of imperfections successfully; any imperfections that
remain are intentionally left to preserve the state of such historical works.

1 MONTH OF
FREE
READING

at

www.ForgottenBooks.com

By purchasing this book you are eligible for one month membership to ForgottenBooks.com, giving you unlimited access to our entire collection of over 700,000 titles via our web site and mobile apps.

To claim your free month visit:
www.forgottenbooks.com/free34697

Similar Books Are Available from
www.forgottenbooks.com

KONINGSMARKE,

OR,

OLD TIMES IN THE NEW WORLD.

"This affair being taken into consideration, it was adjudged that Koningsmarke, commonly called the Long Finne, deserved to die; yet, in regard that many concerned in the affair being simple and ignorant people, it was thought fit to order that the Long Finne should be severely * * * * * * * * * *."

Fragment of Minutes of Council in New-York.

NEW EDITION REVISED AND CORRECTED.

IN TWO VOLUMES.

VOL. I.

NEW-YORK:

PUBLISHED BY HARPER & BROTHERS,

82 CLIFF-STREET.

1834.

BOOK FIRST.

CHAPTER I.

Which, together with all the introductory chapters of this work, is forbidden to our female readers, as containing secrets worth knowing.

In order that our readers and ourselves may at once come to a proper understanding, we will confess without any circumlocution, that we sat down to write this history before we had thought of any regular plan, or arranged the incidents, being fully convinced that an author who trusts to his own genius, like a modern saint who relies solely on his faith, will never be left in the lurch. Another principle of ours, which we have seen fully exemplified in the very great success of certain popular romances, advertised for publication before they were begun to be written, is, that it is much better for an author to commence his work, without knowing how it is to end, than to hamper himself with a regular plot, a succession of prepared incidents, and a premeditated catastrophe. This we hold to be an error little less, than to tie the legs of a

dancing master, to make him caper the more
gracefully, or pinion a man's arms behind his back,
as a preparative to a boxing match. In short,
it is taking away, by a sort of literary *felo de se*,
all that free will, that perfect liberty of imagination and invention, which causes us writers to
curvet so gracefully in the fertile fields of historical
fiction."

Another sore obstacle in the way of the free
exercise of genius, is for a writer of historical novels, such as we have reason to suspect this will
turn out to be, to embarrass his invention by an
abject submission to chronology, or confine himself
only to the introduction of such characters and
incidents as really existed or took place within the
limits of time and space comprised in the ground-
work of his story. Nothing can be more evident
than that this squeamishness of the author must
materially interfere with the interest and variety
of his work, since, if, as often happens, there should
be wanting great characters or great events, coming lawfully within the period comprised in the said
history, the author will be proportionably stinted
in his materials. To be scared by a trifling anachronism, in relation to things that have passed away
a century, or ten centuries ago, is a piece of literary cowardice, similar to that of the ignorant
clown, who should be frightened by the ghost of
some one that had been dead a thousand years.

So far, therefore, as we can answer for ourselves

in the course of this history, we honestly advertise
the reader, that although our hero is strictly an historical personage, having actually lived and died,
like other people, yet in all other respects, not only
he, but every character in the work, belongs entirely to us. We mean to make them think, talk
and act just as we like, and without the least regard
to nature, education or probability. So also as respects the incidents of our history. We intend, at
present, reserving to ourselves, however, the liberty
of altering our plan whenever it suits us, to confine
our labours to no time nor place, but to embody in
our work every incident or adventure that falls in
our way, or that an intimate knowledge of old ballads, nursery tales, and traditions, has enabled us
to collect together. In short, we are fully determined, that so long as we hold the pen, we will
never be deterred from seizing any romantic or
improbable adventure, by any weak apprehension
that people will quarrel with us because they do
not follow on in the natural course, or hang together by any probable connexion of cause and
effect.

Another determination of ours, of which we think
it fair to apprize the reader, is, that we shall strenuously endeavour to avoid any intercourse, either
directly or indirectly, with that bane of true genius,
commonly called common sense. We look upon
that species of vulgar bumpkin capacity, as little
better than the instinct of animals ; as the greatest

pest of authorship that ever exercised jurisdiction
in the fields of literature. ' Its very name is sufficient to indicate the absurdity of persons striv-
ing to produce any thing uncommon by an abject
submission to its dictates. It shall also be our
especial care, to avoid the ancient, but nearly exploded error, of supposing that either nature or
probability is in anywise necessary to the interest
of a work of imagination. We intend that all our
principal characters shall indulge in as many inconsistencies and eccentricities, as will suffice to
make them somewhat interesting, being altogether
assured that your sober, rational mortals, who act
from ordinary impulses, and pursue a course of
conduct sanctioned by common sense, are no better
than common-place people, entirely unworthy the
attention of an author, or his readers.' It is for
this special reason that we have chosen for our
scene of action, a forgotten village, and for our
actors, an obscure colony, whose existence is
scarcely known, and the incidents of whose history are sufficiently insignificant to allow us ample
liberty in giving what cast and colouring we please
to their manners, habits and opinions. And we
shall make free use of this advantage, trusting that
the good-natured public will give us full credit for
being most faithful delineators. Great and mani-
fold are the advantages arising from choosing this
obscure period. The writer who attempts to copy
existing life and manners, must come in competi-

tion, and undergo a comparison with the originals, which he cannot sustain, unless his picture be correct and characteristic. But with regard to a state of society that is become extinct, it is like painting the unicorn, or the mammoth ;—give the one only a single horn, and make the other only big enough, and the likeness will be received as perfect.

Certain cavillers, who pretend to be the advocates of truth, have strenuously objected to the present fashion of erecting a superstructure of fiction on a basis of fact, which they say is confounding truth with falsehood in the minds of youthful readers. But we look upon this objection as perfectly frivolous. It cannot be denied that such a mixture of history and romance is exceedingly palatable ; since, if the figure may be allowed us, truth is the meat, and fiction the salt, which gives it a zest, and preserves it from perishing. So, also, a little embellishment will save certain insignificant events from being entirely lost or forgotten in the lapse of time. Hence we find young people, who turn with disgust from the solid dulness of pure matter of fact history, devouring with vast avidity those delectable mixed dishes, and thus acquiring a knowledge of history, which, though we confess somewhat adulterated, is better than none at all, Besides this, many learned persons are of opinion that all history is in itself little better than a romance, most especially that part wherein historians pretend to detail the secret motives of monarchs

and their ministers.   One who was himself an old
statesman, writes thus :

"How oft, when great affairs perplex the brains
Of mighty politicians, to conjecture
From whence sprung such designs, such revolutions,
Such exaltations, such depressions, wars and crimes;
Our female Machiavels would smile to think
How closely lurking lay the nick of all
Under our cousin Dod's white farthingale."

Such, then, being the case with history, we think
it a marvellous idle objection to this our mode of
writing, to say that it is falsifying what is true, since
it is only sprinkling a little more fiction with it, in
order to render it sufficiently natural and enter-
taining to allure the youthful and romantic reader.

Before concluding this introductory chapter,
which is to be considered the key to our undertaking, we will ask one favour of the reader.   It
is, that if on some occasions we shall, in the course
of this work, appear somewhat wiser in various
matters, than comports with the period of our history, and at other times not so wise as we ought
to be, he will in the one case ascribe it to the total
inability of authors to refrain from telling what
they know, and in the other, to an extraordinary
exertion of modesty, by which we are enabled, at
that particular moment, to repress the effervescence
of our knowledge.

Finally, in order that the reader may devour our
work with a proper zest, we hereby assure him, (in

confidence,) that our bookseller has covenanted and agreed to pay us ten thousand dollars in Owl Creek bank notes, provided the sale of it should justify such inordinate generosity. We will now plunge directly into the thickest of our adventures, having thus happily got over the first step, which is held to be half the battle.

CHAPTER II.

"Peter Piper picked a peck of pickled peppers.
Where is the peck of pickled peppers Peter Piper picked?"

THE curious traveller along the western bank of the Delaware river, will hardly fail to notice some few scattered remains, such as parts of old walls, and fragments of chimneys, which indicate where once stood the famous fort and town of Elsingburgh, one of the earliest settlements of the Swedes in this country. The precise spot these ruins occupy we shall not point out, since it is our present intention to give such an accurate description, that it cannot be mistaken bv a reader of common sagacity.

At the time this history commences, that is to say, somewhere about the middle of the sixteenth century, a period of very remote antiquity considering the extreme juvenility of our country, this important little post was governed by the Heer Peter Piper, a short thickset person, of German parentage, whose dress, rain or shine, week days or Sundays, in peace or war, in winter and summer, was a suit of olive-coloured velvet, ornamented with ebony buttons. A picture still preserved in the Piper family, represents him with a round, and somewhat full face, a good deal wrinkled; sturdy short legs, thin at the ankles, and redundant at the calves ; square-toed shoes, and square buckles of a yellowish hue, but whether of gold or brass is impossible to decide at this remote period. We would give the world, that is to say, all that part of it which is at present in our possession, namely, a magnificent castle in the air, to be able to satisfy the doubts of our readers in respect to the problem whether the Heer Peter Piper wore a cocked hat. But as the painter, with an unpardonable negligence, and a total disregard to posterity, has chosen to represent him bareheaded, we can only say, that his knob was ordinarily covered with a thick crop of hair that curled rather crabbedly about his forehead and ears. It hath been aptly remarked by close observers of human nature, that this species of petulant curl, is almost the invariable concomitant of an irritable, testy, impatient temper, which, as it were, crisps and curls about after a similar manner with the said hair.

Certain it is that, whatever exceptions may occur to the general rule, the Heer Piper was not one of them, he being, as the course of our history will fully substantiate, an exceeding little tyrant, that fell into mortal passions about nothing, broke his nose over every straw that lay in his way, and was seldom to be found in any sort of good humour, except when he had swore vengeance at every soul that excited his wrath. Indeed, to say truth, he was one of those blustering little bodies, who

differ entirely from those who are said to be no
heroes to their valet de chambre, since it was
affirmed of him that he was a hero to nobody else,
but his servants and dependants, whom he bullied
exceedingly. The good people of Elsingburgh
called him, behind his back, Pepper Pot Peter, in
double allusion to the fiery nature of his talk, and
his fondness for the dish known among our ancestors by that name, and remarkable for its high
seasoning. The distich placed at the head of this
chapter, was made upon the Heer Peter, by a wag
of the day, who excelled in alliterative poetry, and
of whom we shall say more anon, if we do not forget it in the multiplicity of adventures we intend to
incorporate into this true history. But as we mean
to leave a good part of our work to the imagination of the reader to supply to the best of his abili-
ties, we will let the character of Governor Piper
develop itself in his future conduct, and proceed
with our story.

One sultry summer afternoon in the month of
July, the Heer Peter having finished his dinner by
one o'clock, was sitting in his great arm chair,
under the shade of a noble elm, the stump of which
is still to be seen, and being hollow, serves for a
notable pig sty, smoking his pipe as was his custom, and ruminating in that luxurious state of
imbecility between sleeping and waking. The
river in front spread out into an expansive lake,
smooth and bright as a looking glass; the leaves

hung almost lifeless on the trees, for there was not a breath of air stirring; the cattle stood midway in the waters, lashing the flies lazily with their tails; the turkeys sought the shade with their bills wide open, gasping for breath; and all nature, animate as well as inanimate, displayed that lassitude which is the consequence of excessive heat.

The Heer sat with his eyes closed, and we will not swear that he was not at this precise moment fast asleep, although the smoke of his pipe still continued to ascend at regular intervals, in a perpendicular column, inasmuch as it was affirmed by Wolfgang Langfanger, and some others of his friends and counsellors, that the Heer Peter did sometimes smoke somewhat instinctively, as a man breathes in his sleep. However this may be, whether sleeping or waking, the governor was suddenly roused by the intrusion of one Lob Dotterel, a constable and busybody, who considered himself, in virtue of his office, at full liberty to poke his proboscis into every hole and corner, and to pry into the secret as well as public actions of every soul in the village. It is astonishing what a triumph it was to Lob Dotterel, to catch any body tripping; he considered it a proof of his vigilance and sagacity. And here, lest the reader should do Master Dotterel wrong, in supposing that the prospect of bribes or fees stimulated him to activity, we will aver it as our belief, that he was governed by no such sordid motive, but acted upon a similar instinct with that of a well-bred pointer dog, who is ever seen wagging his tail with great delight when he brings in game, although he neither expects to be rewarded, or to share in the spoil, at least so far as we have been able to penetrate his motives of action.

Master Dotterel was backed on the occasion aforesaid, by one Restore Gosling, and Master Oldale, keeper of the Indian Queen, the most fashionable, not to say the only tavern, in the village of Elsingburgh. These three worthies had in custody a tall, straight, light-complexioned, blue-eyed youth, who signified his contempt for the accusation, whatever it might be, the constable, Master Restore Gosling, Master Oldale, and the Heer Peter himself, by rubbing his chin on either side with his thumb and fingers, and whistling Yankee Doodle, or any other tune that doth not involve a horrible anachronism.

There are three things a real genuine great man cannot bear, to wit :—to do business after dinner —to be disturbed in his meditations—or to suspect that the little people below him do not think him so great a person as he is inclined to think himself. All these causes combined to put the Heer Peter in a bad humour, insomuch that he privately communed with himself that he would tickle this whistling, chin-scraping stripling.

" Well, culprit," cried the Heer, with a formidable aspect of authority—" Well, culprit, what is your crime? I can see with half an eye you're no better than you should be."

" That's no more than may be said of most people, I believe," answered the youth, with great composure.

" Answer me, sirrah," quoth the Heer, "what is thy crime, I say?"

" Ask these gentlemen," said the other.

" What—eh! you won't confess, hey! an old offender I warrant me. I'll tickle you before I've done with you. What's thy name—whence came you—and whither art thou going, culprit?"

" My name," replied the fair tall youth, "is Koningsmarke, surnamed the Long Finne; I came from the Hoarkill, and I am going to jail, I presume, if I may augur aught from your excellency's look, and the hard names you are pleased to bestow on me."

Nothing is so provoking to the majesty of a great man, as the self-possession of a little one. The Heer Peter Piper began to suspect that the Long Finne did not stand in sufficient awe of his dignity and authority, a suspicion than which nothing could put him in a greater passion. He addressed Master Dotterel, and demanded to know for what offence the culprit was brought before him, in a tone which Lob perfectly understood as encouragement not to suppress any part of the prisoner's guilt. Lob hereupon referred the Heer to Master Oldale, who referred him to Restore

Gosling, who had laid the information. This apparent disposition to shift the *onus probandi* caused additional wrath in the governor, who began to tremble lest the Long Finne might give him the slip, and escape the consequences of his contempt of authority. He thundered forth a command to Gosling to state *all* he knew against the culprit; laying hard emphasis on the word "all."

Master Gosling, after divers scratches of the head, such as my Lord Byron indulgeth in when he writeth poetry, gathered himself together, and said as follows—not deposed, for the Heer held it an undue indulgence to prisoners, to put the witnesses against them to their Bible oath.—Master Gosling stated, that he had seen the young man, who called himself Koningsmarke, or the Long Finne, take out of his pocket a handful of Mark Newby's half-pence, or, as it was commonly called, *Pat's* half-pence, which every body knew was prohibited being brought into the dominions of Sweden, under penalty of confiscation of the money; one half to the informer, and the other half to his sacred majesty, the King of Sweden, Denmark, Norway, and the Goths

" Ho, ho!" exclaimed the Heer, rubbing his hands; "this looks like conspiracy and plot with a vengeance. I should not be surprised if the Pope and the d——l were at the bottom of this." And here we will remind the reader that this was about the time that the manufactory of plots, Popish and Presbyterian, Meal Tub and Rye House, flourished so luxuriantly, under the fruitful invention of Shaftesbury, Oates, Tongue, Dugdale, Bedlow and others. Now the Heer Peter always took pattern after the old countries, insomuch that whenever a plot came out in England, or elsewhere, he forthwith got up another at Elsingburgh, as nearly like it as possible. In one word, he imitated all the pranks, freaks and fooleries of royalty, as an ape does those of a man. At the period, too, which this history is about to commemorate, there were terrible jealousies and heart-burnings betwixt the representatives of royalty in the adjoining or neighbouring colonies of New-Jersey, Pennsylvania, Maryland, New-York, and Connecticut. The different monarchs of Europe, had not only given away with astonishing liberality what did not belong to them, in this new world, but given it away over and over again to different persons, so that it was next to impossible either to settle the boundaries of the various grants, or to ascertain who was the real proprietor of the soil. As to the Indians, they were out of the question. Now, though these tracts were, ninety-nine parts in a hundred, a perfect wilderness, and the number of inhabitants as one to a hundred square miles, yet did these potentates, and especially their governors, feel great solicitude lest they should be in no little time stinted for elbow-room. They were, consequently, always bickering about boundaries, and

.disputing every inch of wilderness most manfully, by protest and proclamation.

The Heer Piper governed a territory by right of discovery, grant, possession, and what not, somewhat larger than Sweden, and which, at the time of this writing, contained exactly (by census) nine hundred and sixty-eight souls, exclusive of Indians. It is therefore little to be wondered at, if, being as he was, a long-headed man, metaphorically speaking, he should begin to look out in time for the comfort of the immense population, which he foresaw must speedily be pressed for room. His jealousy was of course continually squinting at his neighbours, most especially the Quakers at Coaquanock, and the Roman Catholics, who about this time settled at St. Mary's under Leonard Calvert. He therefore pricked up his ears, and smelt a plot, at the very sound of Mark Newby's halfpence, a coin then circulating in West Jersey and Coaquanock, and forthwith set down the Long Finne as an emissary from the Quakers, who, he swore, although they would not fight, had various ways of getting possession of his territories, much more effectual than arms. Moreover, he abhorred them because they would not pull off their hats to the representative of Gustavus Adolphus, and, as he affirmed, were a people who always expected manners from others, although they gave none themselves. In addition to these causes of disgust, it was rumoured, that his excellency the Heer,

being once riding out near Coaquanock, met a
Quaker driving a great wagon, and who refusing
to turn either to the right or to the left, rendered
it necessary for Peter Piper to attempt to pass him,
by the which his buggy was overset, and himself
precipitated into a slough. Let me tell the reader,
that trifles less than these have more than once set
mankind together by the ears, and caused the
rivers of the earth to run red with blood.

Under the influence of these statesmanlike views,
jealousies, antipathies, and what not, the Heer
viewed the possession of such a quantity of Mark
Newby's halfpence as a suspicious circumstance,
and indeed had little doubt, in his own mind, that
the Long Finne had come into the settlement to se-
duce it from its allegiance to the great Gustavus, by
actual bribery. The reader may smile at the idea
of corrupting a community with halfpence, now
when paper money is so plenty that dollars fly
about like may-flies in the spring, and that it sometimes actually takes a hundred of these to purchase
a man's conscience. But we will make bold to tell
him, his smile only betrays an utter ignorance of
the simplicity of those times, when a penny was
deemed equal to six white and four black wampum; and a tract of land, larger than a German
principality, was at one time purchased for sixty
tobacco-boxes, one hundred and twenty pipes, one
hundred Jews-harps, and a quantity of red paint.
It hath been shrewdly observed, that the value of

money regulates the consciences of men, as it does
every other article of trade, so that the suspicion
of Governor Piper was not quite so ridiculous as
many ignorant readers may be inclined to suppose
at first sight.   This explanation we afford gratui-
tously, hinting at the same time, that as it is no
part of our plan to make things appear probable,
or actions consistent, we shall not often display a
similar disposition to account for what happens.

"Long Finne," said the Heer, after considerable
cogitation—" Long Finne, thou art found guilty of
suspicion of traitorous designs against the authority
of his sacred majesty, Gustavus Adolphus of Sweden, and in order that thou mayest have time and
opportunity to clear up thy character, we sentence
thee to be imprisoned till thine innocence is demonstrated, or thou shalt confess thy guilt."

By this time half the village, at least, was collected, as is usual on these occasions, when they
flock to see a criminal, as porpoises do about a
wounded mate, not to succour, but to worry him.
The whole assembly were struck with astonishment at the wisdom of Governor Piper's decision,
which they looked upon as dictated by blind justice
herself.   Not so the Long Finne, who like most unreasonable persons, that are seldom satisfied with
law or justice when it goes against them, seemed
inclined to remonstrate.   But the Heer, whose
maxim it was to punish first and pity afterward,
forthwith commanded him to be quiet, quoting his

favourite saying, " Sirrah, if we both talk at once, how are we to understand one another ?"

As they were taking him from the presence of the governor to convey him to prison, the tall, fair youth, turned his eye mildly, yet significantly towards the Heer, and pronounced in a low voice the words, "Caspar Steinmets." " What! who! whose name did you utter ?" exclaimed his excellency in great agitation—

"Caspar Steinmets"—replied the youth.

" What of him '—rejoined the Heer.

" I am his nephew"—replied the Long Finne. " The friend of your youth would be little obliged to you, could he see you hurrying the son of his bosom to a prison, because he possessed a handful of Mark Newby's halfpence."

" Pish !" cried the Heer—" I never heard that old Caspar Steinmets had a nephew, and I don't believe a word of it."

" He had a sister, who married a gentleman of Finland, called Colonel Koningsmarke, against the wishes of her friends. She was discarded, and her name never mentioned. On the death of both my parents, my uncle adopted me, but he died also, not long after you sailed for the new world.—Look, sir, do you know this picture ?"

" Blood of my heart," exclaimed the Heer, contemplating the picture, " but this is old Caspar Steinmets, sure enough ! Ah ! honest, jolly old Caspar ! many a time hast thou and I drunk, fought and raked together, in bonny Finland! But for all that, culprit, thou shalt not escape justice, until thou hast accounted to me for the possession of this picture, which hath marvellously the appearance of stolen goods."

"Stolen goods, sir!" interrupted the fair youth, passionately; but, as if recollecting himself, he relapsed again into an air of unconquerable serenity, and began to whistle in an undertone.

"Ay, marry, stolen goods! I shall forthwith commit thee to prison, and retain this picture till thou provest property, and payest all charges. Take him away, master constable."

The youth seemed about to remonstrate, but again, as if suddenly recollecting himself, remained silent, shrugged his shoulders, and quietly submitted to be conducted to the prison, followed by the crowd, which usually, on such occasions, volunteers as an honourable escort to heroes of the bridewell and quarter sessions. But nothing could equal the triumph of Lob Dotterel on this occasion, who looked upon the establishing of a man's innocence to be lessening the importance of a constable, who, as he affirmed, derived dignity and consequence in exact proportion to the crimes of mankind.

Having despatched this weighty affair, the Heer Piper knocked the ashes out of his pipe, and returned to his gubernatorial mansion, with a full resolution of communicating the whole affair to the Chancellor Oxenstiern.

CHAPTER III.

"There was an old woman, and what do you think?
She liv'd upon nothing but victuals and drink:
Victuals and drink were the chief of her diet,
And yet this old lady could never be quiet."

Mother Goose's Melodies.

Now the long shadows of the trees that stretched almost half way across the river, began gradually to disappear, as the sun of summer sunk behind the hills that rose gradually and gracefully one above another westward of the renowned, or soon to be renowned, village of Elsingburgh. The toils of the day being finished, some of the villagers were sitting at the door of Master Oldale's castle, smoking and telling tales of wars in the old countries, or dangers encountered in the new.

The maids and matrons were, some, busily preparing the ponderous supper; others, milking the cows; and others, strolling with their sweethearts on the bank of the river, under the ancient elms, full sorely scarified with names, or initials of names, and true lovers' knots, the rude, yet simple emblems of rustic love. Dame Parlet, the hen, with all her cackling brood, nestled for the night upon the shady boughs; the domestic generations of two-legged and four-legged animals were about seeking their various lodgings, and the careful hind was seen unchaining the trusty and powerful mastiff, the faithful guardian of himself, his children, wife, and all his treasures, from surprise, in the solitude of the night, when the wild wolf, and the Indian equally wild, were often heard to yell the quavering knell of danger and death.

Every object began gradually to approximate to that rural repose and happy quiet which characterizes the evening of a country hamlet, among a people of simple and virtuous habits.

In one word, it was just the period betwixt daylight and dark, when the Heer Piper, as affirmed at the end of the last chapter, returned to his mansion, to indulge himself in his accustomed stout supper, which usually consisted of a tankard of what is called *hard* cider, a species of beverage, which goes down a man's throat like a sharp sword, and which the sturdy Heer called emphatically man's cider, it being an unquestionable demonstration of manhood to be able to drink it, without causing the eyes to start out of the head. To this was usually added a mess of pepper-pot, with heaps of meat and vegetables, among which figured, in all the dignity of a national dish, the execrable and ever-to-be-avoided *sour-krout* dire. All these luxuries of the day were spread on the table, and waited his coming, in company with the members of the household.

The first of these which we shall introduce in due form to the reader, was the lady Edith Piper, only sister to his excellency the governor—a per-

son of ominous notability, who, on the death of the
Heer's wife, had taken command of the establishment, and, if report says true, of Governor Piper
into the bargain. She was, in the main, a good
sort of a body, and of a most public-spirited disposition, since she neglected the affairs of the Heer,
to attend to those of every body else in the village.
She knew every thing that happened, and a vast
many things that 'never' happened. And we will
venture to pledge our veracity as historians, that
there never were but two secrets in the village,
from the time of Madam Edith's arrival, to the
day of her final extinction. One was the year of
the lady's birth—the other we do not care to dis-
close at present, being anxious to convince the
world that we too can keep a secret as well as
other folk.

To do the good lady no more than justice, she
was not ill-natured, although her thirst after knowledge was somewhat extreme; nor did she ever
make any bad use of the village tittle-tattle, which
came to her ears. She never repeated any tale
of scandal, without at first impressively assuring
her hearers that she did not believe one word of
it, not she; she merely told the story, to show what
an ill-natured world it was that they lived in.
Madam Edith was supposed to maintain her authority over the Heer Piper, more by dint of talking
incessantly, than through the agency of fear. When
she had a point to gain, she never abandoned it;

and if, as often happened, the governor walked out in a pet to avoid her importunities, she would, on his return, resume the argument just where it was left off, with astonishing precision. In process of time she worried him out, and, from long experience of the perseverance of the dame, as well as the inefficacy of resistance, Governor Piper came at last to a quiet submission to be tyrannized over within doors, being resolved to make himself amends by tyrannizing without. The Vrouw Edith, who, we neglected to premise, was never married, not being able to find any body in the old or new world good enough for her, was, in sober truth, a considerable talker, although the same regard to veracity impels us to the confession that she was not always understood by her hearers. Taking it for granted, that every body was as anxious about every body's business as herself, she gave them credit for as much knowledge, and was perpetually indulging in hints, innuendoes, and scraps of biography, which puzzled her friends worse than the riddle of the Sphinx. Thus she generally alluded to her acquaintances in old Finland, by their christian names, and detailed the various particulars incident to nurseries, kitchens, &c. as if the whole universe felt an interest in the subjects of her biography. In one word, she was a thin, short little body, dressed in high-heel'd shoes, a chintz gown, with flowers as large as cabbages, and leaves like those of the palm, together with a long-tabbed lawn cap,

which, on great occasions, was displaced for one
of black velvet, fitting close to the head, and tied
under the chin. Of her voice, it may be affirmed
that it was as sharp as the Heer's favourite cider.

The only being in the governor's establishment
that could hold a candle to aunt Edith, as she was
usually denominated, or who ventured to exchange
a shot in the war of words with her, was a certain
mysterious, wayward, out-of-the-way creature, who
was generally reputed to be an equal compound of
fortune-teller and witch. She was by birth an
African, and her general acceptation was that of
Bombie of the Frizzled Head. Bombie was a
thick, squat thing, remarkable for that peculiar
redundancy of figure, so frequently observed in
the ladies of her colour and country. Her head
and face were singularly disproportioned to her
size, the first being very small, and the latter, proportionably large, since it might with truth be
averred, that her head was nearly all face. The
fact was, that nature had given her such a redundancy of broad flat nose, that in order to allow of
any eyes at all, she was obliged to place them on
either side of the head, where they projected almost as far, and as red as those of a boiled lobster.
This gave her an air of singular wildness, inasmuch
as it produced the peculiar look called 'staring,
which is held to be the favourite expression of that
popular class of lately created beings who stand
in a sort of a midway between witches, goblins,

fairies, and devils, and are an odd compound of
them all.

Bombie of the Frizzled Head, was so surnamed
on account of her hair, which was distinguished
by that peculiar and obstinate curl, which, together
with the accompanying black complexion, are held
to be the characteristics of the posterity of Cain.
Age had, at this period, bent her body almost
double, seamed her face with innumerable wrinkles,
and turned her hair white, which contrasted singularly with her ebony skin. But still she exhibited one of the peculiarities of this unhappy race,
in a set of teeth white as the driven snow, and
perfect as the most perfect ever seen through the
ruby lips of the lass the reader most loves. And
if the truth must be told, her tongue seemed to be
as little injured by the assaults of time as her teeth.
She was, in fact, a desperate railer, gifted with a
natural eloquence that was wont to overpower the
voice and authority of aunt Edith, and drive the
Heer Piper from his sternest domestic resolves.

The tyranny of Bombie's tongue was, however,
strengthened in its authority by certain vulgar
opinions, the more powerful, perhaps, from their
indefinite nature and vague obscurity. It was said
that she was the daughter and the wife of an African
king, taken in battle, and sold to a trader who carried her to St. Barts, where she was hought by the
Heer Peter Piper, who whilome figured as Fiscal
of that fruitful island, from whence she accompa-

nied him first to Finland, and afterward to the new world. Rumour, that progeny of darkness, distance, and obscurity, also whispered that she of the Frizzled Head could see into the depths of futurity; was acquainted with the secrets of sticking crooked pins, and throwing invisible brickbats; and dealt in all the dread mysteries of *Obi*. These suspicions were strengthened, by the peculiar appearance and habits of the Frizzled Head, as well as by the authority of certain instances of witchcraft that happened about this time in the East, as recorded by the learned and venerable Cotton Mather, in his book of wonders, the Magnalia.

Like the owl and the whippoorwill, she scarcely ever, was seen abroad except at night, and, like them, she was supposed to go forth in the darkness, only to bode or to practise ill. With her short pipe in her mouth, her horn-headed stick in her hand, she would be seen walking at night along the bank of the river, without any apparent purpose, generally silent, but occasionally muttering and mumbling in some unknown gibberish that no one understood. This habit of prowling abroad at night, and at all times of the night, enabled her to attain a knowledge of various secrets of darkness that often seemed the result of some supernatural insight into the ways of men. Indeed, it has been, or it may be shrewdly observed, that he who would see the world as it really is, must watch like the mastiff that bays the moon, and sleeps but in the sunshine.

When at home, in the Heer's, kitchen, she never slept except in the day time; but often passed the night, wandering about such parts of the house as were free to her, apparently haunted by some sleepless spirit, and often stopping before the great Dutch clock in the hall. Here she might be seen, standing half double, leaning on her stick, and exhibiting an apt representation of age counting the few and fleeting moments of existence. Her wardrobe consisted of innumerable ragged garments, patched with an utter contempt for congruity of colouring, and exhibiting the remnants of the fashions of the last century. On particular occasions, however, Bombie exhibited her grand costume, which consisted of a man's hat and coat, and a woman's petticoat, which combination produced a wild, picturesque effect, altogether indescribable. In justice to the Heer, we must premise, that it was not his fault that Bombie was not better clad, for he often gave her clothing, with which no one ever knew what was done, as she was seldom seen in any thing but a multiplicity of rags.

Though, to appearance, exceedingly aged and infirm, the *Snow Ball,* as Governor Piper used to call her, was gifted with an activity and power of endurance, that had something almost supernatural in it, and which enabled her to brave all seasons, and all weathers, as if she had been the very statue of black marble she sometimes seemed, when standing stock still, leaning on her stick and contemplating the silent moon. She had a grandson, of whom we shall say more by and by. At present we will leave the Heer to finish his supper, as we mean to do our own presently, not wishing to burthen the reader with too much of a good thing, which is shrewdly affirmed to be equivalent to a thing which is good for nothing.

CHAPTER IV.

" The rose is red, the violet blue,　　*l*
　The gilly-flower sweet, and so are you.
　These are the words you bade me say,
　For a bonny kiss, on Easter day."
Mother Goose's Melodies.

WE left our hero, at the conclusion of the last chapter save one, quietly on his way to prison, in the custody of Lob Dotterel, the vigilant high constable of Elsingburgh. The reader may perhaps wonder at the spiritless acquiescence with which the Long Finne submitted to the decision of the Heer Piper, as well as to the safe conduct of the constable. Now, though it is in our power, by a single flourish of the pen, to account for this singularity, we are too well acquainted with the nature of the human mind, to deprive our history at the very outset of that indescribable interest which arises from the author's keeping to himself certain secrets, which, like leading strings, as it were, conduct the reader to the end, in the hope of at length being fully rewarded by a disclosure, a hope in which, it must be confessed, he is often sadly disappointed, seeing it is much easier to knit, than to unravel a mystery. Suffice it to say that the tall youth was quietly conducted to prison, apparently without either caring much about it himself, or exciting the compassion of a single soul in the village.

But it was not so.—There was one heart that
melted with sympathy, and one eye that shed a
solitary tear, to see so interesting a youth thus, as
it were, about to be buried alive, upon so vague
and slight a suspicion: That heart, and that eye,
beat in the bosom, and sparkled in the brow of as
fair a maid as ever the sun shone upon in this new
world, whose sprightly daughters are acknowledged
on all hands to excel in beauty, grace, and virtue,
all the rest of the universe. The daughter, the
only daughter, nay, the only offspring of the Heer,
was sitting in the low parlour window that looked
out upon the green sward, where that puissant
governor used to smoke his afternoon's pipe in
pleasant weather, when the vigilant high constable
brought in the tall, fair prisoner. Her eye was
naturally attracted by a face and figure so different
from those she had been accustomed to see in the
village, and being sufficiently near to hear his ex-
amination, she was struck with wonder and curiosity, two sentiments that are said to be inherited
by the sex, in a direct line from grandmother Eve.

Those readers, ay, and writers too, who happen
to know as much of human nature as the head of
a cabbage, are aware of the electrical quality of
any excitement that springs up in the heart, in a
situation, and under circumstances, where objects
of interest are rare, and there is no variety to at-
tract us from the train of thought and feeling, which
such objects inspire. In early youth, and just at

that blooming period of spring, when the bud of
sentiment begins to expand its leaves to the zephyr
and the sun, it often happens, that the memory and
the fancy will both combine to rivet in the mind, a
feeling lighted by a single spark, in a single moment, and make its impression almost indelible.

It was thus, in some degree, with the fair and
gentle daughter of the Heer, whose light azure
orb, the colour of the north, seemed destined to
conquer all hearts in the new world, as her blue-
eyed ancestors did the old with their invincible
arms.   She had never yet seen, except in dreams,
since she entered her teens, a being like the Long
Finne, who, contrasted with the sturdy boors
around her, not even excepting her admirer Othman Pfegel, was an Apollo among satyrs.   Christina, for so was she called, had indeed some remote
recollection of a species of more polished beings,
such as, when a little girl, she had seen in Finland;
but the remembrance was so vague as only to enable her in some degree to recognise the vulgarity
and want of refinement of the Sunday beaux of
Elsingburgh.

The heart, the pure, warm, social heart of a girl
of seventeen, may be said to be like the turtle
dove, which pines in the absence of its mate, and
fills the wilderness of the world with its solitary
moanings.   It waits but to see its destined coun-
terpart, to tremble and palpitate; and if its first
emotions are not rudely jostled aside, or overpow-

ered by the distraction of conflicting objects, and
the variety of opposing temptations, they will become the governing principle of existence during
a whole life of love.

Koningsmarke was, in truth, a figure that might
have drawn the particular attention of a lady
whose eyes were accustomed to the finest forms
of mankind. He was nearly, or quite six feet
high, straight, and well proportioned, with a complexion almost too fair for a man, and eyes of a
light blue. His hair was somewhat too light to
suit the taste of the present day, but which, to one
accustomed, like Christina, to associate it with ideas
of manly beauty, was rather attractive than other-
wise.

With these features, he might have been thought
somewhat effeminate in his appearance, were it
not that a vigorous, muscular form, and a certain
singular expression of his eye, which partook somewhat of a fierce violence, threw around him the
port of a hardy and fearless being. This expression of the eye, in after times, when their acquaint-

vague and indefinite suspicions of his character,
and fears of its development, which the fair Christina could seldom wholly discard from her bosom.
The dress of the youth, though not fine nor splendid,
was of the better sort, and in excellent taste, except that he wore his ruff higher up in the neck
than beseemed.

The person whose appearance we have thus
sketched, as might be expected, excited a degree
of interest in the maiden, sufficiently powerful to
have impelled her to actual interference with the
Heer, in favour of the prisoner, had it not been
for that new-born feeling, which, wherever it is
awakened in the bosom of a delicate and virtuous
female, is accompanied by a shrinking and timid
consciousness, that trembles lest the most common
courtesies, and the most ordinary emotions, may
be detected as the offspring of a warmer feeling.
Besides this, the fair Christina knew from experience that though her father loved her better than
all the world besides, there was one thing he loved
still better, and that was, the freedom of his sovereign will and pleasure, in the exercise of his authority as the representative of Gustavus Adolphus
of Sweden.   The Heer, in fact, never failed to
resent all interference of this nature on the part of
the ladies of his household, always accompanying
his refusal by some wicked jest, or some reflection
upon people's not minding their own business.
Christina, therefore, remained quiet in her seat, and
accompanied the fair, tall youth to prison, with the
sigh and the tear heretofore commemorated.

The prison formed one side of the square, at the
opposite extremity of which was placed the governor's palace, as he called it, videlicet, a two-story
brick house, with a steep roof, covered with fiery
red tiles, lapping over each other like the scales

of a drum fish. The bricks which composed the walls of the palace were of the same dusky hue of red, so that the whole had the appearance of a vast oven, just heated for a batch of bread. Agreeably to the fashion of the times, the house was of little depth, the windows of the same room opening to both front and rear; but then it made up in length what it wanted in depth, and when not taken in profile, had a very imposing appearance. Exactly opposite, at a distance of about thirty yards, was the prison, also of brick, with small windows, having ominous iron bars, and other insignia shrewdly indicative of durance vile. One part of the building was appropriated to the accommodation of persons who had the misfortune to fall under the guilt of suspicion, like the Long Finne; and in the other portion, was the great court room, as it was pompously called, where the Heer met, as was his custom, to consult with his council, and do just as he liked afterward, as practised by the potent governors of that day. In truth, these little men were so far out of the reach of their masters, that they considered themselves as little less than immortal, and often kicked up a dust for the sole purpose of showing their authority.

The governor's mansion, and the court-house or jail, were the only brick buildings in the village, the rest consisting of wooden edifices of round logs for the vulgar, and square ones, filled in with mortar, for the better sort. These were huddled

close together round the square, for two special
reasons; one, that they might be the more easily
included in the strong palisade, 'which had been
raised about the town for security against any
sudden irruption of the savages; the other, that
no ground might be wasted in laying out the place,
which, in the opinion of the longest heads, was so
advantageously situated, that every foot of land
must be of immense value some day or other.
Vain anticipations! since the place is now a ruin,
and the colony no more; yet such is the usual fate
of all the towering hopes of man! The houses
we speak of, were all nearly of the same size and
fashion, and equally dignified by an enormous
chimney of brick, which appertained to the house,
or more strictly speaking, to which the house
seemed to appertain, and which being placed outside of the wall instead of inside, for the purpose
of affording more room to the family, gave the
mansion somewhat the relative appearance of a
wren house stuck up against the side of a chimney.

In this veritable jail, we have just described,
the Long Finne was consigned by Lob Dotterel,
and received by the Cerberus who guarded it, and
who, finding the emoluments of his office consider-
ably inadequate to maintain a family, of some eight
or ten children, generally worked at his trade of
carpenter abroad, leaving the keys of the prison in
the hands of his wife. The latter was popularly
considered the better man of the two, and currently

reported not to fear devil or dominie, in fair open daylight.

Master Gottlieb Swaschbuckler's vocation might be said to be almost a sinecure, since, notwithstanding Lob Dotterel's vigilant police, the 'prison was, during the greater part of the year, undignified by a single inhabitant, save the jailer and his family. And here we cannot but express our mortification, that, notwithstanding the vast pains taken since that time to improve the mind and morals of mankind, and the astonishing success of all the plans laid down for that purpose, there should be such a singular and unaccountable increase of the tenants of jails, bridewells, penitentiaries, and such like schools of reformation. So extraordinary indeed is the fact we have just stated, that we feel it incumbent upon us, to request of the reader a little exertion of that generous credulity, by which he is enabled to gulp down the interesting improbabilities of our modern romances.

Dame Swaschbuckler was, consequently, delighted at the appearance of the Long Finne, having been some time without any body but her husband and family upon whom to exercise her authority, and holding, as she did, that a prison without a prisoner was, like a cage without a bird, utterly worthless and uninteresting. She was resolved to entertain him in her best manner, and accordingly showed him into a room, the doors of which were twice as thick, and the windows ornamented with double the number of bars, of any other in the whole building.

Having thus accommodated our hero with board and lodging, we shall pause a moment in order to cogitate what we shall say in the next chapter.

CHAPTER V.

"Who comes here ?   A grenadier.
What d'ye want ?   A pint of beer.
Where's your money ?   I forgot.
Get you gone, you drunken sot."
                                    Mother Goose's Melodies.

WE neglected to mention, not foreseeing that it might be necessary to the course of our history, that the Heer Piper, when he pronounced sentence upon the Long Finne, did also at the same time declare, all that portion of Mark Newby's half-pence which he carried about him, utterly forfeited, one half to the informer, the other to the crown of Sweden.   It was accordingly divided between Restore Gosling and the governor, as the representative of majesty.

The Long Finne accordingly entered the prison, without that key which not only unlocks stone walls, but also the flinty hearts of those who are wont to preside within them.   His pockets were as empty as a church on week-days.   When, therefore, the next morning he felt the gnawings of that insatiate fiend, whom bolts, nor bars, nor subterranean dungeons, suffice to keep from tagging at the heels of man, and ventured to hint to dame Swaschbuckler that he had some idea of wanting his breakfast, that good woman promptly desired him to lay down his dust, and she would procure him a breakfast fit for Governor Piper himself.

"But I have no dust, mother, as you call it," replied the youth.

"What, no money!" screamed out the dame; "*der teufel hole dich*, what brought thee here then."

"Master Lob Dotterel," replied he.

"And thou hast no money—*du galgen schivenkel*," roared the dame.

"Not a stiver, nor even one of Mark Newby's halfpence," responded the Long Finne.

"Then thou gettest no breakfast here," cried the mistress of the stone jug, "except *der teufel's braden*. It would be a fine matter truly, if every *galgengefallener spitzbube* were to be maintained here in idleness, at the expense of the poor." So saying, she waddled indignantly out of the room, shutting the door after her with great emphasis, and turning the key with a quick motion, indicating wrath unappeasable.

Dinner-time came, but no dinner; supper-time came, but no supper; for it ought to be premised, that it was one of the Heer Piper's maxims, that the less a criminal had to eat in prison, the more likely he would be to come to a speedy confession of his crime. He therefore made no provision for persons committed on mere suspicion. Most people, we believe, happen to be aware of the vast importance of eating and drinking, not only as a very simple means of supplying the wants of nature, but likewise as creating certain divisions of time, whereby that venerable personage is disarmed of

half his terrors, and the desperate uniformity of
his pace agreeably interrupted. Accordingly, when
the night came, and nothing to eat, the Long Finne
began to feel not a little tired of his situation. He
paced his solitary room in silent vexation, occasionally stopping at the window, which fronted the
governor's palace, and gazing wistfully at the
figures which passed backwards and forwards
about his little parlour. As he stood thus contrast-
ing the cheerful aspect of the palace with his dark,
noiseless prison, and his own solitary starving state,
he beheld them bringing in the Heer's supper, and
his bowels yearned. The contrast was more than
he could bear; he flung himself upon the straw in a
corner of the room, and communed with himself in
the bitterness of his heart; he drank his own tears in
the extremity of his thirst, and finally sinking under
weakness, and the emotions of his heart, fell asleep.

From this last refuge of misery and hunger the
Long Finne was awakened by a loud peal of thunder,
that seemed to have shattered the prison into atoms.
On opening his eyes, the first object he beheld, by
the almost unceasing flashes of lightning, was a
figure standing over him, half bent, and leaning
upon a stick, muttering and mumbling some unintelligible incantation. Her eyes seemed like coals of
fire, dancing in their deep sockets, and her whole
appearance was altogether, or nearly supernatural.

" Who, and what are you, in the name of God ?"
cried the Long Finne, starting up from his straw.

"I am a being disinherited of all the rights, and heir to all the wrongs to which humanity is prone. I was born a princess in one quarter of the globe —I was brought up in another, a beast of burden. I am here the slave of man's will, the creature of his capricious tyranny." The voice of the apparition was hollow, and rung like a muffled bell.

"And what brought thee here at this time of the night," replied the youth, "and such a night too!"

"The thunder and the lightning, the storm and the whirlwind, are my elements; night to me is day; and when others sleep, the spirit that is unseen in the morning, the guilty that fear, and the injured that hate the light and the face of man, go forth to warn the living, to indulge the bitterness of their hearts, or to commit new crimes."

"Away!—I know thee now; thou art Bombie of the Frizzled Head—I know thee now," replied the youth.

"And I too KNOW THEE," hollowly rejoined the figure—"I know thee, Long Finne. Thou comest here for no good; thou art here to stab the sleeping innocent—to ingraft upon the tree of my master's house the bitter fruit of guilt and misery. I am sent here to prevent all this. I come with food, and the means of freeing thee from thy prison. Follow me, and go thy ways, never to return."

"I will stay here and die," bitterly exclaimed the fair youth. "I am an outcast from my native land —a hunted deer, to whom neither the woods, the waters, nor the air afford a refuge. Whither shall I go? Nor white man nor red man will shield me from that which follows me every where—from the worm that never dies, the fire that is never quenched. No—I will stay here and perish." He flung himself recklessly on the floor, and covered his face with his hands.

"Stay here and perish!" replied the Frizzled Head, scornfully. "Thus does the coward white man quail and whimper, when he hath done that which his abject spirit dare not look in the face. He that hath the courage to commit a crime, should have the courage to face its consequences. Coward, arise and follow me."

"No—I will die here."

"And perish hereafter," cried the black mystery, setting down a little basket beside the youth. "Farewell; but be careful what thou doest. Wherever thou goest I will follow; whatever thou doest I shall know; and if, under cover of night and solitude, when thou thinkest that no mortal eye seeth thee, thou darest to do ill, my eye shall be upon thee, and my spell wither thy resolves. Beware!"

Thus saying, she departed, and sorry are we to say, it was in a manner somewhat unworthy her mysterious dignity; for she passed out at the door, and locked it after her. The Long Finne lay ruminating for some time on what he had seen and heard; but at length his curiosity inspired him with the idea of examining the basket, the contents of which drove every thing else out of his head. And here we might tamper with the reader's curiosity, and affect that mystery with which certain writers are wont so unmercifully to torment their readers. But we scorn all such vulgar arts of authorship, and honestly confess that the Long Finne was struck dumb by the sight of an excellent supper, which he attacked with great vigour, after the manner of men that have fasted much and prayed little.

The visit of the Frizzled Head was, after this, repeated nightly, and the supper with it, doubtless with the connivance of dame Schwaschbuckler, whose husband, being a great politician, usually spent the first part of the night in getting foxed at Master Oldale's shrine, and the other part in sleeping himself sober at home.

In truth, the weeping blood of woman's heart seldom beats with a stronger feeling of pity, than it now began to do in the bosom of the fair Christina. She was observed to be often at the window of her chamber, which fronted the prison, through whose bars she had a dim and indistinct view of the tall, fair youth, pacing backwards and forwards in his narrow bounds, and sometimes stopping before the grates, where he would lay his hand on his heart, and bow his head profoundly, as if to thank her for her charity to a poor wanderer. Sometimes, in the evening, he would play on a little flageolet which he managed exquisitely, and occasionally sing portions of the tender and popular airs of her country, among which she often distinguished the following couplet:—

"Mauern machen kein gefængniss,
Und eisersne stangen kein kæfig;"

which seemed to her expressive of the triumph of mind over time and circumstance.

- Those who have studied the heart of woman, and read in its ruddy pages how prone it is to pity, and how naturally it passes from pity to a warmer feeling, we trust will give us credit for some little regard to probability, when we venture to hint, that the little simple village girl had not long indulged in the one, till she began to feel the approaches of the other.

The moment she became aware of this change in her feelings, all the pleasure she had hitherto felt in administering, through the instrumentality of Bombie, to the wants of the prisoner, vanished. An indescribable sensation of awkward embarrassment possessed her, whenever she applied to the sibyl to carry his daily supply. And the blush which accompanied the application, was the silent, yet sure testimony that she was now acting under the impulses of a new feeling, which she dared not avow.

The conduct of the Frizzled Head increased this embarrassment.—The sibyl every day discovered more and more unwillingness to go on her nightly errand of charity, and was perpetually pouring forth mystical prophecies and denunciations.

" I will not," said she at last, " I will not pamper

the wolf that he may be preserved to devour the
innocent lamb. I have seen what I have seen, I
know what I know. There is peril in the earth,
the sea, and the air, yet the young see it not till it
comes, and when it comes they know not how to
escape.—I will go to the prison no more."

"And the youth will be left to perish with hunger," replied the young damsel, sadly.

· "Let him perish!" exclaimed the Frizzled Head.
"The guilty die, that the innocent may live;' for
wickedness is the strength of the lion, and the cunning of the tiger combined. Enough can it ac-
complish of mischief without my assistance—I will
go no more."

"In the name of Heaven, what meanest thou,"
asked the trembling girl, " by these fearful hints
of danger? Who is the wolf, and who the lamb,
that thou shouldst thus thwart me in my errand of
compassion?"

"I have seen what I have seen—I know what
I know," replied the sibyl. " The warning that is
given in time, is the word which is howled out in
the wilderness. Better were it for one of my colour
to be dumb than speak evil of one of thine. But I
have seen what I have seen—I know what I know."

This was all poor Christina could get out of the
old mystery, and that night the Long Finne went
supperless to his straw, with the thought lying like
lead upon his heart, that he was now forgotten and
forsaken by all the world.

BOOK SECOND.

CHAPTER I.

Which the courteous reader is advised to skip over, unless peradventure he loves truth better than fiction.

THE farther we advance in our history, the more do we perceive the advantages of extempore writing. · It is wonderful, with what a charming rapidity the thoughts flow, and the pen moves, when thus disembarrassed of all care for the past, all solicitude for the future. Incidents are invented or borrowed at pleasure, and put together with a degree of ease that is perfectly inconceivable by a plodding author, who thinks before he speaks, and stultifies himself with long cogitations as to probability, congruity, and all that sort of thing, which we despise, as appertaining to our ancient and irreconcilable enemy, common sense. It may in truth be affirmed of this new and happy mode of writing, that it very often happens, that it causes less trouble to the author than to the reader, the latter of whom not unfrequently, most especially if he is one of those unreasonable persons who suppose that nature and probability are necessary parts of an historical novel, will be sorely puzzled to find out the motive of an action, or the means by which it was brought about.

But whatever may be the profit of the reader, certain it is, that of the author is amazingly enhanced by the increased velocity attained by this new mode of writing. Certain plodding writers, such as Fielding, Smollet, and others, whom it is unnecessary to name, wrote not above three or four works of this sort in the whole course of their lives; and what was the consequence? They lived from hand to mouth, as it were, for want of a knowledge of the art of writing extempore ; and were obliged to put up with an immortality of fame, which they could never enjoy. Instead of making a fortune in a few years by the power of multiplying their progeny, they foolishly preferred to pass whole years in the unprofitable business of copying nature, and running a wild-goose chase after probability.

And here we will take occasion to dilate a little more copiously upon the great advantages, which may reasonably be expected from the apt disposition of authors to imitate this mode of writing without plan, and mixing the opposite ingredients of truth and falsehood. Books must of necessity multiply so fast, that every village, and every individual will, after a year or two from their publication, be able to purchase a library for little or nothing, as is the case with a vast many popular works, which in a little time come upon the parish, as it were, and are sold to whoever will·afford· them house-room. Thus will knowledge be wonderfully disseminated, and every body come to know, not only what did happen, but also what did not happen, in the various ages and countries of the world. Nay, we should not be at all surprised if, under the increased facilities afforded by this happy invention of the extempore, every person should in time become his own author, and furnish his own library, at the expense of paper and printing only : and without any trouble, of thought whatever.

We could dilate infinitely on this copious subject, did we not feel confident that the reader must be by this time extremely impatient to pursue our story. We will therefore content ourselves with expressing a firm belief, that, as religion and politics are already taught through the medium of fiction, it will not be long before the sciences generally, both moral and physical, will be inculcated in the same manner. We confidently predict the delightful period when history will be universally studied through the medium of impossible adventure, and truth sweetly imbibed in the fascinating draughts of improbable fiction; when young people shall make chemical love, and gain each other's affections by the irresistible force of lines, tangents, affinity, and attraction; and when the consummation, of all things shall happen, in young children being taught their A. B. C. by the alluring temptation of being able to read novels, instead of appealing to their low-born appetites through the vulgar medium of gingerbread letters.

CHAPTER II.

" Sing, sing—what shall I sing ?
The cat's run away with the pudding-bag string."
Mother Goose's Melodies.

WHILE Dan Cupid was shooting his arrows with
such effect from the windows of the prison, to those
of the palace, and so back again, the Heer Piper
and Madam Edith were taken up with other
weighty affairs, that prevented any interference
with the young people on their part. His excellency was confined to his room with a fit of the
gout; a disorder, which, according to the theory
of a waggish friend of ours, naturally resolves itself
into three distinct stages in its progress. The first
is the swearing stage, wherein the patient now and
then indulges himself with cursing the gout lustily.
The second, called the praying stage, is when he
softens down his exclamations into "O, my G—d!"
or " bless my soul !" and the like. The third, and
worst of all, is the whistling stage, during which
the patient is seen to draw up his leg with a long
wh—e—e—w ! accompanied by divers contortions
of visage. This gout, the Heer was wont to say,
was the only inheritance he received from his father,
who left one of his sons the estate without the gout,
and the other the gout without the estate ; which,

in the opinion of Governor Piper, was a most unjust distribution.

During these attacks, the Heer's natural irascibility of temper was, as might be expected, greatly increased, insomuch, that if any one came suddenly into the room, or opened the door with a noise, or walked heavily, so as to shake the floor, he would flourish his crutch most manfully, and exclaim, " *der teufel hole dich, der galgen schivenkel;*" or, if it happened to be Bombie of the Frizzled Head, " *das tonnerwetter schlage dich kreutzeveis in den boden,*" one of his most bitter denunciations. Indeed, the only person allowed to approach him was the fair and gentle Christina, whose soothing whispers, and soft, delicate touch, seemed to charm away his pains, and lull his impatient spirit into temporary rest. At such times, he would lay his hand gently on her head, cry "God bless thee, my daughter," and close his eyes in quiet resignation. Such is the balm of filial affection! such the divine ministration of tender, duteous woman!

On these occasions, the gentle Christina would glide out of the room like the sylph of divine poetry, and seat herself at her window, there to indulge her newly awakened feelings, and sigh over the captivity of the handsome stranger.

In the mean while Madam Edith was busily employed in the investigation of some stories circulating in the village, and especially in getting at the bottom of a report concerning a certain love

affair, current at that time. Any thing of this sort
gave her the fidgets in a most alarming degree;
for she resembled Queen Elizabeth in this respect,
that the marriage of any one within the sphere of
her influence, gave her a similar sensation with
that cherished by the dog in the manger, who
would not eat himself, nor suffer any body else
to eat. However this may be, aunt Edith was
so completely monopolized by out-door business,
that she paid little attention to what was going on
within, and suffered her niece to do as she pleased,
without interruption.

In process of time, the Heer Piper became
sufficiently recovered to limp about with crutch
and velvet shoe, and take an interest in the affairs
of the village, which, in his opinion, had suffered
exceedingly during his illness. One day, by chance,
he bethought himself of the Long Finne, and pondered how it came to pass that he had not been
brought to confession by this time. He had now
been imprisoned nearly eight-and-forty hours, and
Governor Piper held him to be a tough piece of
humanity, if he did not, by this time, feel somewhat
compunctious, under the combined influence of
solitude and hunger. He forthwith determined
to call the fair tall youth before his privy council,
and accordingly, despatched his trusty messenger
Cupid, grandson to the incomprehensible Bombie
of the Frizzled Head, to summon them together.

This Cupid was a gentleman of colour, as the

polite phrase is, about four feet and a half high, with an ebony complexion, flat nose, long wrinkled face, small eyes sunk in his head, a wide mouth, high cheeks, bushy eye-brows and eye-lids, small bandy legs, of the cucumber outline, and large splay feet, which, it is affirmed, continued to increase in size, long after every other part of him had done growing. In short, he was, to use the phrase of our southern brethren, " a likely fellow."

Cupid was reckoned the worst chap in the whole village, being always at the head of every species of juvenile mischief ; and, if report spoke truth, had more than once attempted to set fire to the houses of persons against whom he had a pique. Lob Dotterel's fingers itched to get hold of him ; but the awe in which he, together with the rest of the villagers, stood of his grandmother's supernatural powers, checked the surprising vigilance of the high constable, and saved Cupid's bacon more than once. The boy, who was now supposed to be about eighteen, notwithstanding his diminutive size, was as obstinate as a mule, as mischievous as a monkey, and as ill-natured as a bull-dog. Punishment was lost upon him, and kindness thrown away. Neither one nor the other ever drew a tear from his eye, an acknowledgment of his fault, or promise of future amendment. Belonging, as he did, to a race who seem born to endure, both in their native Africa, and every where else, he suffered in silence, and revenged himself in the obscurity of the night, by the exercise of a degree' of dexterous cunning, which is often seen among those whose situation represses the impulses of open vengeance.

The only gleams of affection or attachment ever exhibited by this dwarfish and miserable being seemed called forth by his grandmother, and an old Swedish cur, belonging to the Heer. If any one insulted or worried, as children are wont to do, the old woman, or the old dog, the rage of the dwarf was terrible, and his revenge bounded only by his means of mischief. Twice had he cut open the head of a village urchin guilty of this offence, with a large stone, and once was on the point of stabbing another, if he had not been prevented. His grandmother doted on him with that obstinate and instinctive affection, which is so often called forth by those very qualities that render its object hateful or contemptible in the eyes of the world. As to old *Grip*, the dog, he would obey nobody, follow nobody, fawn on nobody, or bite, or wag his tail at the bidding of any earthly being, except the black dwarf Cupid, but on all occasions condescended to obey the behests of this his puissant master.

Then came, in due time, Wolfgang Langfanger, the pottee-baker, Ludwig Varlett, the shoemaker, who, if he ever heard the old proverb *ne sutor*, &c. despised it with all his heart, and Master Oldale, fat and plump as a barrel of his own spruce beer, all good men and true, and members of his majesty's council in the good town of Elsingburgh. After the different "how doon ye's" had been exchanged, and the Heer had given a full, true, and particular history of his late fit of the gout, he opened his business, and Lob Dotterel, who always instinctively attended on these occasions, was despatched for the Long Finne. In the mean time, the Heer and his council lighted their pipes, and took their seats with most imposing dignity. Master Lob fulfilled his duty in the twinkling of an eye, and the Long Finne appeared in the high presence, with pretty much the same air of indifference as before, and with a rosy complexion, which puzzled the Heer not a little, till he resolved the thing into a blush of conscious guilt.

" Well, *henckers knecht*," said the Heer, "have you come to your senses by this time ?"

" I am no *henckers knecht*," replied the Long Finne, " and I have never been mad, all my life."

" *Der teufel hole dich*," exclaimed the Heer, waxing wroth ; " dost think to brave it out with me in this manner, *der ans dem land gejacter kerl?* Where gottest thou that handful of Mark Newby's halfpence? answer me that, *der teufels braden*."

" Ask Lob Dotterel," replied the youth ; " he saw me receive them in change for some rix-dollars, from a stranger who passed through the village."

" *Der teufel !*" exclaimed the Heer, and thereupon the three members of the council gave a

simultaneous puff extraordinary, expressive of
astonishment.

" Hark ye, Lob Dotterel," said the Heer, "didst
see the Long Finne receive this money in change
from the stranger ?"

" I did," replied master high constable, who began to feel his prisoner slipping through his fingers.

" *Verflucht und verdamt !*" exclaimed the Heer,
dashing the ashes from his pipe in a mortal passion;
"and why didst not tell me so before, *der galgen
schivenkel ?*"

" 'Twant my business," quoth Lob ; " your excellency always tells me not to put in my oar, till
I am called to speak."

" Put him to his Bible oath," said the Heer, who
held that, though the oath of a witness was not
necessary to the committing of a person to jail, yet
was it indispensable to his release. Whereupon
Wolfgang Langfanger, the pottee-baker, pulled out
of his breeches pocket, a marvellously greasy little
square book with silver clasps, which, having first
rubbed bright on the sleeve of his coat, he handed
to the Heer. Lob Dotterel was then incontinently
put to his corporal oath, and confirmed the account
which the prisoner had given of his coming into
the possession of such a quantity of Mark Newby's
halfpence.

" *Der galgen schivenkel !*" exclaimed the Heer,
shaking his crutch at Lob Dotterel, who looked
rather sheepish, and, for that matter, so did his

excellency. However, he gathered himself together, and forthwith pronounced so discriminating
a judgment on the case, that, had not the town of
Elsingburgh been extinct long ago, it would, doubt‑
less, have been remembered to this day in the tra‑
ditions of the inhabitants. Mustering together his
recreant, runaway dignity, he decided, that he
should divide his judgment into two parts. And
first, as he, Koningsmarke, surnamed the Long
Finne, was acquitted of treasonable practices in
regard to the possession of Mark Newby's halfpence, he should be released from prison. Secondly,
that inasmuch as he had not been able to give a
good account of himself, and of his motives for
coming to the village, he should be again remanded
to jail, on suspicion of certain designs, which, as
yet, did not sufficiently appear to the satisfaction
of his majesty's government. The rest of the council signified their approbation, according to custom,
by saying nothing ; for it ought to have been premised that the Heer Piper, as the representative
of majesty, held, that though bound to consult his
council, he was not bound to pay any attention to
their opinions. In fact, it was his maxim, that a
council was of no other use to a governor, than
to bear the blame of any unlucky or unpopular
measure.

As Lob Dotterel placed his withering paw on
the shoulder of the Long Finne, that mysterious and
unaccountable youth took occasion to except to the

governor's assertion that he had not been able to give a good account of himself.

" If your excellency is not satisfied, I will begin again, and give you the history of my family, from the flood, in which some of my ancestors were doubtless drowned, to the present time, when"—

" When," interrupted the Heer, " one of their posterity, at least, is in some danger of being hanged. Begone, *der ans dem land gejacter kerl.* Away with him to prison."

The Long Finne bowed with a sly air of ironi- cal submission, shrugged his shoulders, and quietly submitted to the guidance of the high constable of Elsingburgh.

CHAPTER III.

"Lady bird, lady bird,
    Fly away home,
  Your house is on fire,
  Your children will burn."

Mother Goose's Melodies.

It was on a Saturday afternoon that the Long
Finne was remanded to prison, in the manner detailed in the last chapter. The gentle Christina
wept, and wrung her hands; for he must know
little of the heart of a woman, who cannot comprehend to what a degree the exercise of those
good offices conferred upon the Long Finne,
through the instrumentality, of Bombie, together
with the pity she felt for his unmerited imprisonment, had softened the heart of this gentle girl
towards the tall, fair youth. She besought the
Frizzled Head to carry him his supper as usual;
but that ancient sibyl pertinaciously replied with
her eternal sing song of "I have seen what I have
seen—I know what I know."

The blue-eyed damsel of the north could not
sleep that night, which turned out dark and dismal.
She sat at her window, and the death-like silence,
unbroken by a single sound, save the howling of
the north-east wind, added to her feelings of deso-
lation. Through the black void that separated the

prison and the palace, she could see the Long Finne
pacing past the grated window, from which poured
the light of his lamp.   When it disappeared, supposing the youth had gone to rest, Christina threw
herself on her bed, and after long and troubled
wakefulness, sunk into an unquiet sleep, haunted
by dreams even more doleful than her waking
thoughts.

She was roused by a glaring light shining full
into the room, with a brightness that astonished and
alarmed her. Starting up, and running to the
window that looked towards the prison, she saw a
sight that froze her blood into horror. 'The bars
of the prison seemed like those before a red-hot
furnace, and all within exhibited a fiery redness.
Anon, the flames poured forth from the windows
of the keeper's apartment, in glaring volumes,
advancing and receding as the different currents
of air obtained a mastery. To utter a loud shriek,
to run to her father, and to awaken the whole household, was the work of a moment; and in a few
minutes afterward, all was noise and confusion in
the village of Elsingburgh.

Every man, woman, child, and dog in the town
was out, lending assistance to the uproar, and im-
peding, in some way or other, the attempts made
by a few persons, not quite out of their senses, to
stop the progress of the flames. Tongue cannot
describe, nor imagination conceive, the discordant
cries of "fire, fire," the shrieks of women, and the

howls of dogs, that mingled in the mighty uproar, and drowned the voices of those who attempted to give directions for preventing the fire from spreading into the village.

With much difficulty they forced the outer door, which led to the keeper's apartments, where they found that trusty blade, Gottlieb Schwashbuckler, and his wife, fast asleep, in spite of the shriekings of the little urchins within, and the uproar without. The truth is, that Saturday night was generally devoted by Master Gottlieb and his fat rib, to certain loving tipplings, which commonly ended in their both going to sleep, just on the spot where they took the last glass together. On this night, the fire in an adjoining room, which served as parlour and kitchen, had been left burning, for the purpose of drying Madam Schwashbuckler's best, and indeed only, chintz gown, (an article which conferred, at that time, no little distinction on the possessor,) together with certain other articles of dress, intended for the husband and children the ensuing Sunday. Besides these, there was in the chimney corner, a quantity of light wood, which Master Gottlieb, who smelt a storm that night, had collected together for the use of the morrow. Either the clothes had taken fire, and communicated to the dry wood, or the latter had first caught, and communicated to the former; for this is one of those knotty difficulties, which even authors, who know so many secrets, are often unable to resolve.

Be this as it may, when the door was burst open, the flames had so far advanced, that a few minutes more and it had been all over with the ancient family of the Schwashbucklers. As the door opened, the little brood rushed out like so many caged partridges; but it was with no little difficulty that the sleeping pair were made to comprehend their situation, and with still more that they were got out of the building, it being their pleasure to stay and dispute which was to blame for this catastrophe.

The opening of the large door which fronted the direction from which the wind was blowing, having given an impulse to the flames, they almost instantaneously communicated to the only staircase that led to the upper story of the prison. It was now in vain to attempt saving the building, and accordingly, one part of the community were employing themselves in sprinkling the roofs of such houses as were most exposed to the flakes of fire, which now began to soar into the air, while others were quietly looking on in gaping wonderment, sometimes watching the reflection of the flames, that at one moment spread upwards on the bosom of the dark sky, and at another receded, leaving them darker than before. Others were adding to the horrors of the scene, by wailings, and cries of fire, fire, although by this time, every one was collected from far and near.

At this moment the mysterious Bombie rushed

among the crowd, crying out, in a voice that overpowered the infernal uproar,—"Shame on the pale-faced race! They will let one of their colour perish in the flames, without essaying to relieve him, as if he were one of those ye call the posterity of the first murderer!"

"There is nobody in the prison!" exclaimed half a hundred voices.

"There is, I tell you," replied the sibyl. "Look! see ye not a shadow, passing among the lights in yonder room? See ye not that he is putting forth his hands through the grates, imploring assistance? See ye not how he tries to wrench the iron from its fixture in the last effort of despair. He is innocent—at least," muttered she to herself, "he is innocent of the crime for which he is here—would I could say of all others.".

"A ladder! a ladder!" cried half a hundred voices at once. But alas! there was no ladder to be had long enough to reach the window.

The person of master Gottlieb Schwashbuckler was then searched for the key of the room where the prisoner was confined, and all his pockets turned inside out to no purpose. At last that worthy, after rubbing his eyes, scratching his head, and yawning half a dozen times, avowed his firm belief that he had locked the room carefully last evening, and as carefully left the key sticking in the key-hole. Several attempts were now made, by different persons, to ascend the staircase and unlock the door, which was not more than two paces from it; but they all returned without success, some with their hair, singed, others with scorched hands, and almost suffocated; in short, all now declared that relief was entirely hopeless.

Bombie now advanced a little before the rest, leaned upon her horn-headed stick, and cried out with an almost supernatural voice—" Koningsmarke !"

, " I hear"—answered a voice from within.

" Koningsmarke—thy fate is in thine own hands; all human help, save thine, is vain. Exert thy strength upon the door, or upon the iron bars. Thou art strong, and thou art desperate ; exert thyself and be free, or perish—as thou deservest," said the sibyl, ending in a low mutter.

At that moment there was a crash within the building, and the disappearance of the youth was announced by a groan from the spectators, whose noisy exclamations now sunk into a horrible silence. A minute or two after, he appeared again, at the window, having employed the interval of his disappearance in attempting, in vain, to force the door. Now he made a desperate effort at the bars of one of the windows, but they resisted his strength. " The other ! the other !" cried the sibyl.

He essayed the other without success. " 'Tis in vain," cried the youth, in despair. " I perish here ; remember ! remember !"

" Remember thou !" shrieked the old woman ; " Remember that the dove of thy Christian legend went forth thrice, ere she found what she sought. Try once again."

He tried again, but in vain—the bars shook, but did not yield.

" Once more," cried she, " for the sake of thy benefactress."

He essayed again with convulsive strength— the bars shook—moved—the wall in which they were inserted trembled—gave way—and the whole fell into the room. A shout of triumphant humanity announced the event. " Jump—jump for thy life !"; cried out one and all, for that was the only way to escape. Koningsmarke hung for a moment, with his hands, from the side of the broken window, and at length, letting himself go, fell to the ground insensible

CHAPTER IV.

"And why may not I love Johnny?
And why may not Johnny love me?
And why may not I love Johnny,
As well as another body?"

Mother Goose's Melodies.

WHERE was the fair and gentle daughter of the Heer, while what we have detailed in the last chapter was passing? That innocent and tender-hearted maiden, checked by the innate sense of propriety, which is the truest safeguard of virtue, and restrained by the timidity of new-born affection, remained at home in a state of the most painful anxiety. She despatched the old sibyl Bombie to bring her information, and then stood at her window, watching with increasing agitation, the progress of the devouring element. She could distinguish, by the glaring light, the stranger youth, sometimes standing at the window, as if imploring his rescue, and every time he disappeared, a hope arose in her bosom, that the door had been opened for his escape. But he returned again, and again, while at every new disappointment, her agitation increased; until at length, when she heard the crash of the falling staircase, and saw a shower of burning cinders rise into the air, the blood rushed to her heart, and her senses became for awhile suspended.

KONINGSMARKE.   **69**

With the first moment of returning animation, the fair Christina beheld the black sibyl standing over her, muttering one of her incomprehensible spells, in a low and sepulchral voice. " Is he safe," asked the maiden, fearfully.

" The wolf is again abroad, and let the innocent lamb beware," replied the Frizzled Head.

" What in the name of Heaven meanest thou, by thy parable of the wolf and the lamb ! Be silent, or tell all thou knowest, I beseech thee," said the startled girl.

" The slave cannot witness against the master, nor the colour I bear, testify against thine. I have seen what I have seen—I know what I know. Sleep out the rest of this night in the sleep of innocence, for no one knows but it may be the last."

So saying, the mysterious monitor bade her young mistress good night, and retired, leaving poor Christina to muse with painful curiosity on her dark and inscrutable oracles.

In the mean time, the Heer Piper had been apprised of the situation of the Long Finne, who, as we have before stated, was taken up insensible, after his fall from the window of the prison. Though a testy, impatient little man, the Heer was, at the bottom, neither ill-natured nor malignant. He could not reflect on the imminent danger to which his suspicions had exposed the stranger youth, without a painful feeling of remorse, or contemplate his present forlorn and desolate condition, without compassion. Yielding to his feelings, he directed that the Long Finne should be brought to his palace, where he was placed on a bed, and every means in their power used for his recovery. It was for some time doubtful whether the soul and the body had not parted forever ; but at length the youth opened his eyes with a long-drawn sigh, then shut them again for a few moments, during which, nature seemed to struggle between life and death. At length, however, the desperate contest was over ; the colour gradually came back into his cheeks, and he seemed to recognise the Heer, who had watched his revival with no little solicitude.

The recovery of the Long Finne, who was sorely bruised with his fall, was slow and gradual, but it was at last completed, and he became a man again. Unwilling any longer to trespass on the hospitality of the Heer, the youth one day took an opportunity to express his deep and indelible sense of the obligations he owed to the Heer and his family, his inability to repay them for the present, his hope that Providence would one day put it in his power, and finally, his resolution to depart on the morrow. The Long Finne had now been an inmate of the palace, somewhat more than a month, and during all that time experienced unvarying kindness. It is one of the most noble and delightful characteristics of our nature, that whatever may be our first motive for bestowing kindness on a fellow creature, we cannot continue long to do so, without in time

coming to love the object of our benevolence.
Mankind, indeed, are prone to become ungrateful,
and to feel uneasy at the sight of a benefactor ; but
the bestower of benefits is never without his reward in the complacency of his feelings, and the
approbation of his own heart.' There is, too, a
social feeling in human nature, which is nurtured
by domestic intercourse, and which gradually dis-
sipates hasty and unfounded prejudices, since it is
hardly possible to live in the same house with a
person whose manners are tolerably conciliating,
without feeling something of that species of neighbourly good will, which, after all, is the strongest
cement of society.

It was so with the Heer Piper, who felt no little
complacency of spirit, when he looked back upon
the various claims his late kindness had given him
and his, on the gratitude of the youth. When,
therefore, he heard the proposition for to-morrow's
departure, it was with something like a feeling of
dissatisfaction.

"Why, hang it, Long Finne," he exclaimed, "I
hope there is no ill-blood between us about the
affair of Mark Newby's halfpence—eh l".

"I were ungrateful if I remembered that," said
the youth. "Thou hast buried it for ever under
the recollection of a thousand kindnesses. I remember nothing, but that I owe my life, worthless
as it is, to you."

"Well, well," replied the Heer, "I will tell thee

what. Thou sayest thou art friendless? and without money, and where wilt thou find either one or the other, in this wilderness?"

"Alas! I know not," replied the youth; "but it is better to go forth in search of new friends, than to tire our old ones"

"*Der teufel hole dich*," cried the fiery and puissant Heer; "who told thee thy old friends were tired of thee? are my household negligent, or do I treat thee with any more ceremony than a kitten? 'Slife Master Long Finne, but that the jail is unluckily burnt down, I'd clap thee up again, for such a false suspicion, I would—*der teufel hole dich*."

"But I have not been used to live on charity" rejoined the youth.

"Charity!" furiously exclaimed the Heer. "Charity! *verflucht und verdamt!* why, 'sdeath, am not I governor of this territory, and can't I take a man into my palace out of my own free will and pleasure, without being accused of charity, and having the matter thrown into my teeth, *der teufel!* Hark ye, Long Finne, either stay in my house till I can provide for thee, or by the immortal glory of the great Gustavus, I'll clap thee up between four stone walls, if I build another jail on purpose."

"Thou shalt not need," replied the Long Finne, smiling; "I will not run away from you. Perhaps I may make myself useful, at least in time of danger. I was once a soldier, and if the savages should ever attempt the fort, I may repay some of my obligations."

"Very well," quoth the Heer; "away with thee; and hark ye, if I hear any thing more about that d—d charity, I'll set that mortal speechifier, the *Snow Ball,* at thee, for I perceive thou art more afraid of her confounded smoked tongue than of der teufel." As the Heer said this, he looked round rather apprehensively, as if to see whether the Snow Ball was not within hearing, knowing full well that if he affronted her, she would spoil his pepper-pot for him at supper.

The Long Finne bowed, left the high presence of the representative of majesty, and from thence went to a place where he was pretty certain of meeting the charming Christina, who had ministered to his sick bed, like a guardian sylph— Pshaw! like a gentle, compassionate, sweet-souled woman! who is worth all the sylphs that ever sung or flitted in the vacuum of a poet's brain.

"Art thou going away to-morrow?" asked Christina, with her blue eye cast to the earth.

"No," replied the youth with a smile; "thy father threatens me with building a new prison if I talk of departing. I will stay, and at least, lose my liberty more pleasantly."

That evening, the Long Finne and the gentle Christina walked on the white sand beach, that skirted the wide expansive river, over whose placid

bosom the south wind gently sailed, and the moon-
beams sprinkled a million of little bright reflections,
that danced on the waves, as they broke in gentle
murmurs on the pebbly shore.　Night, and silence,
those tongue-tied witnesses of the lover's innocent
endearments, the seducer's accursed arts, the murderer's noiseless step, the drunkard's reel, and the
houseless wretch's wanderings—night, and silence,
created that solitude, in which happy, youthful lovers, see nothing but themselves, and forget that
they exist not alone in this world.　The almost
noiseless monotony of the waves, appearing, breaking, vanishing one after another, like the evanescent
generations of man ; the splash of the sturgeon, at
long intervals, jumping up, and falling back again
into the waters ; these, and other soothing sounds,
enticed them to wander far down the shore, out of
sight and out of hearing of the village.

. All at once they were startled by a voice from
the bank above them, exclaiming—not, " O, yes !
O, yes !" or " Hear ye ! Hear ye !" but singing the
following wild, mysterious strain :

> They sat all in a lonely grove ;
> 　Beneath the flowers were springing,
> And many a bonny bird above,
> 　His blithesome notes was singing.
>
> With harmless innocence of look,
> 　And eyes so sweetly smiling,
> Her willing hand he gently took,
> 　The first step to beguiling.

A kiss he begg'd—she gave a kiss,
   While her cheek grew red and flushing;
For o'er her heart the tide of bliss,
   With thrilling throb was rushing.

He's gone away, to come no more;
   And she who late so smiling,
The blush of bonny youth aye wore,
   Now mourns her sad beguiling.

Her hope is cross'd, her health is lost,
   For ever and for ever;
While he, on distant billows toss'd,
   Returns to her—no, never!

She wanders lonely to and fro,
   Forsaken and forsaking;
And those who see her face of wo,
   See that her heart is breaking.

The voice and the figure were those of the Frizzled Head, who possessed the musical talent, so remarkable a characteristic of her African race, and who had been taught this song by Master Lazarus Birchem, heretofore commemorated, to whom she had given many a dish of pepper pot, for his prize poetry. She was seen by the moonlight, standing half bent, leaning on her stick, at the top of the bank, looking like an old witch, if not something worse. As she finished this long ditty, she cried out, in a sepulchral tone, " Miss Christina, you're wanted at home ; the supper is ready, and the pepper-pot is getting cold. The wolf is abroad, let the lamb beware. I have seen what I have seen—I know what I know."

So saying, she mounted her stick, which we are rather afraid was not a broomstick, and capered off like an ostrich, half running, half flying. The young couple returned to the palace, and Christina remarked that the Long Finne uttered not a word during the rest of the walk.

CHAPTER V.

"Arthur O'Bower has broken his band,
And he comes roaring up the land ;
King of Scots, with all his power,
Never can turn Sir Arthur O'Bower."
Mother Goose's Melodies.

THE summer passed away, and autumn began to hang out her many-coloured flag upon the trees, that, smitten by the nightly frosts, every morning exhibited less of the green, and more of the gaudy hues that mark the waning year in our western clime The farmers of Elsingburgh were out in their fields, bright and early, gathering in the fruits of their spring and summer's labours, or busily employed in making their cider ; while the urchins passed their holydays in gathering nuts, to crack by the winter's fire. The little quails began to whistle their autumnal notes ; the grasshopper, having had his season of idle sport and chirping jollity, began now to pay the penalty of his thoughtless improvidence, and might be seen sunning himself, at mid-day, in melancholy silence, as if anticipating the period when his short and merry race would be run. Flocks of robins were passing to the south, to seek a more genial air ; the sober cattle began to assume their rough, wintry coat, and to put on that desperate appearance of ennui, with which all nature salutes the approach of winter. The little bluebird alone, the last to leave us, and the first to return in the spring, sometimes poured out his pensive note, as if bidding farewell to the nest where it had reared its young, as is set forth in the following verses, indicted by Master Lazarus Birchem, aforesaid, erewhile flogger to the small fry of Elsingburgh :—

Whene'er I miss the bluebirds chant,
By yon woodside, his favourite haunt,
I hie me melancholy home,
For I know the winter soon will come.

For he, when all the tuneful race
Have sought their wintry hiding place,
Lingers, and sings his notes awhile,
Though past is nature's cheering smile.

And when I hear the bluebird sing
His notes again, I hail the spring;
For by that harbinger I know,
The flowers and zephyrs soon will blow.

Sweet bird! that lovest the haunts of men,
Right welcome to our woods again,
For thou dost ever with thee bring
The first glad news of coming spring.

All this while, the fair Christina and the tall youth were left to take their own way; to wander, to read, to sing, and to look unutterable things, unobserved and unmolested, save by the mysterious and incomprehensible warnings of the black sibyl of the Frizzled Head, who, whenever she met them, was continually dinning in their ears the eternal sing-song of "I have seen what I have seen—I know what I know." At such interruptions, the eye of the Long Finne would assume that fearful expression which, we have before observed, had startled the fair Christina, and which, now that she felt a stronger interest in the youth, often occasioned a vague sensation of fear, that caused her many a sleepless night.

The situation of our little blue-eyed Finlander became every day more painful and embarrassing. The consciousness of her growing interest in the Long Finne, the obscurity of his character, 'the equivocal expression of his eye, and the mysterious warnings of the Frizzled Head, all combined to produce a sea of doubts and fears, on which her heart was tossed to and fro. At times she would resolve to alter her deportment towards the youth, and banish him her father's house, by a harsh and contemptuous indifference. But here love, in the form of pity, interfered. Poor, friendless, and unknown, where should he find a refuge, if banished from the village? He would be forced to seek the woods, herd with the bands of Indians, and become himself the worst of savages, a white one. At other times she determined to consult aunt Edith. But that good lady, as we observed before, had too much to attend to abroad, to mind affairs at home ; and was so smitten with a desire to do good on a great scale, that her sympathies could never contract themselves to the little circle of the domestic fireside. Her father next presented himself to her

mind, as her natural guardian and counsellor. But
the Heer, though he loved her better than pipe or
pepper-pot, was a testy, scolding little man; apt
to speak rather more than he thought, and to
threaten more than he would do. Hence the tender apprehensive feelings of a delicate girl, thus
circumstanced, shrunk from the idea of being perhaps roughly assailed in the outset, although, in the
end, she might meet with affectionate sympathy.

The Heer, at this time, was sorely environed
with certain weighty cares of state, that perplexed
him exceedingly, and added not a little to the irri-
tability of his temper. He was engaged, tooth and
nail, in a controversy about boundaries, with his
neighbour William Penn, who, it is well known,
was a most redoubtable adversary in matters of
paper war. Two brooks, about half a mile apart
from each other, and having nothing to distinguish
them, caused great disputes, with respect to the
boundary line between the territories of Coaquanock and Elsingburgh. Trespasses, on either side,
occasioned mutual complaints, and though the Heer
Piper fell into a passion and swore, the other kept
his temper, and the possession of the territory in
dispute besides. In order to settle this affair, it was
proposed to send an envoy to Elsingburgh, on the
part of those of Coaquanock, and accordingly he
made his appearance, about this time, at this renowned capital.

Shadrach Moneypenny, as he was called, for

excellencies and honourables did not fly about like hail-stones, at that time, as now, was a tall, upright, skin-and-bone figure, clothed from head to foot in a suit of drab-coloured broadcloth; a large hat, the brim of which was turned up behind, and without any appendage that approached to finery, except a very small pair of silver buckles to his high-quartered shoes. Yet, with all this plainness, there was a certain sly air of extreme care in the adjustment of his garments, in accordance with the most prim simplicity, that shrewdly indicated friend Shadrach thought quite as much of his appearance as others, who dressed more gaudily to the eye. The Long Finne, who was somewhat of a mischievous wag at times, affirmed that the worthy envoy looked very much as if he had gone through the same process of washing, clear-starching and ironing, with his precise band and rigid collar. Shadrach Moneypenny rode a horse seventeen hands high, and proportionably large and jolly in his other dimensions, which afforded a perfect contrast to the leanness of his rider; so that one likened them unto Pharaoh's dream, another to king Porus and his elephant, and various were the jokes cracked upon Shadrach and his big horse, as they entered the village. It was with much ado that Lob Dotterel could prevent the bad boys from jeering the stranger, as they sat in the road, busily employed in making dirt pies, in joyful anticipation of the coming of the Christmas holydays.

The governor receivéd the envoy in full council.
—And here it occurs to us, that we have not properly introduced these distinguished persons to the
reader, an omission which shall be duly supplied,
before we proceed one step farther in our history.

Wolfgang Langfanger, the pottee-baker, was
the greatest smoker, and of course the greatest
man in the village, except the representative of
majesty himself. He was, in time past, considered
among the most prosperous and thriving persons
in all the territories of New Swedeland, being an
excellent baker of stone pots, some of which remain to this day in the houses of the descendants
of the ancient inhabitants, beautifully lackered with
green flowers, and bearing the initials of W. L.,
which would doubtless sorely puzzle future anti-
quaries, were it not for this true history. What
he earned, he saved; and being manfully assisted
by his spouse, within doors, he gradually waxed
wealthy, insomuch, that he every year built either
a new hen-house, pig-sty, or the like, and white-
washed his garden fence, in spring and fall. But
from the period in which he arrived at the unex-
pected honour of being of the king's council, his
head seemed turned topsy-turvy, and his good
helpmate's inside out. Wolfgang fell into such a
turmoil, respecting the affairs of the great Gustavus, who, at that time, was carrying the reformation on the point of his sword into Germany, that
he never baked a good pot afterward; while his

wife began to scorn whitewashing fences, and
churning infamous butter. The very next Sunday,
she took the field at church, dressed in a gown of
the same piece, and a cap of the same fineness,
with those of Madam Edith, to the great scandal of
Dominie Kanttwell, and the utter spoiling of aunt
Edith's pious meditations for that day. More than
that, Wolfgang began to frequent master Oldale's
house, where he talked politics, drank ale, smoked
his pipe till the cows came home, and got the reputation of a long-headed person that saw deep into
futurity.

Sudden wealth and sudden honour ruineth many
an honest man. We have seen a prize in the lot-
tery, and an election to the dignity of assessor or
alderman, spoil some of the most worthy trades-
men in the world. Thus was it with Wolfgang
Langfanger, who spent his money, and neglected
his business, till at length he had not a rix-dollar
left, and his reputation, as a pot-baker, was ruined
for ever. At the time we speak of, he lived, sometimes upon credit, sometimes by his wits; the
former he employed in running up long scores
with master Oldale; the latter, in suggesting divers
famous schemes for the improvement of Elsingburgh, whereby the value of property would be
trebled, at least, and every soul suddenly become
rich: but of these anon. Still, the dignity of his
office supported him in the midst of his poverty;
for, even at that time, it was possible for a great

man to live sumptuously, and spend other people's money, without its being considered as any disparagement to his wonderful talents and honesty.

The second member of his majesty's council was Othman Pfegel, who had some pretensions to an old Swedish title of Baron, which lay dormant, somewhere under the polar ice. He professed, what was called, a sneaking kindness for the fair Christina, and was highly in favour with the governor, with whom he was very sociable, insomuch that they would smoke for hours together, without uttering a word. Truth, however, our inflexible guide in this history, obliges us to confess, that the only overt act of love he ever committed against the heart of the fair Christina, was, always puffing the smoke of his pipe towards that fair damsel, whenever she was in the room, which was held a sure indication of the course to which his inclinations pointed. Othman was considered a most promising youth, seeing that he had arrived at such a distinguished honour at the early age of forty-eight; and there were those who did not scruple to hint that he might one day come to be governor of Elsingburgh. Othman and the Long Finne were sworn enemies; the one, evincing his hostility, by comparing his rival to a barn-door in a frosty morning, which is always smoking; the other, by taking no notice, whatever, of his rival, in his presence, and making divers reflections upon him when absent.'

The third member of the great council of New

Swedeland was Ludwig Varlett, a wild, harem-scarem, jolly fellow, lazy as a Turk, idle as a West India planter, and so generous, when he had money, that he was often obliged to be mean for the want of it. He held prudence, economy, necessity, and the like, to be words of Indian origin, and whenever any one used them in his presence, would exclaim, " Eh ! what ?—pru—I don't understand it, it's Indian." Counsellor Varlett dealt liberally, in a great variety of singular expletives and epithets, peculiar to himself, and which were at every one's service. But then he would consign people to the bitterest punishments in this way, with such a good-humoured eccentric vehemence, that nobody ever thought of giving him credit for being in earnest, or taking offence at his discourse.

But with all this bad habit, Counsellor Ludwig was, in the main, a good-natured man, who took the world as it went ; charitable to the poor, whom he would relieve with a hearty malediction ; one, in fact, who would have deserved great credit for his liberality, had it not been too often exercised at the expense of his creditors. He never looked beyond the present moment, and was accustomed to anathematize Counsellor Langfanger's schemes of improvement, which were always founded on distant views of future advantage. The consequence was, that the latter got the reputation of a very long-headed person, while honest Ludwig was stigmatized as a short-sighted fellow.

When Shadrach Moneypenny appeared before the council of New Swedeland, the first offence he gave was omitting either to make a bow, or pull off his hat, to the great annoyance of Governor Piper; who was as great a stickler for ceremony as the Emperor of China, or the secretary of state, in a republic, where all are equal. The Heer fidgeted, first one way, then another, made divers wry faces, and had not Shadrach been a privileged person, on the score of his plenipotential functions, would have committed him to the custody of Lob Dotterel, to be dealt with contrary to law.

In the mean time, Shadrach stood bolt upright, with his hands crossed before him, his nose elevated towards the ceiling, and his eyes shut. At length be snuffled out—

"Friend Piper, the spirit moveth me to say unto thee, I am come from Coaquanock to commune on the subject of the disputes among our people and thine, about certain boundaries between our patent and the pretended rights of thy master."

"Friend Piper—pretended rights," repeated the Heer, muttering indignantly to himself. "But hark ye, Mr. Shadrach Mesheck and the d—l, before we proceed to business, you must be pleased to understand, that no man comes into the presence of the representative of the great Gustavus, the bulwark of the Protestant religion, without pulling off his hat."

"Friend Piper," replied Shadrach, standing in

precisely the position we have described—"Friend
Piper, swear not at all. Verily, I do not pull off
my hat to any one, much less to the representative
of the man that calleth himself the great Gustavus,
whom I conceive a wicked man of blood, one who
propagateth religion with the sword of man instead
of the word of Jehovah."

" *Verflucht und verdamt !*" exclaimed the Heer,
in mortal dudgeon : "the great Gustavus, the bulwark of the Protestant faith, a man of blood!
Der teufel hole dich ! . I swear, you shall put off
your hat, or depart, without holding conference
with us, with a flea in thine ear."

"Swear not at all," replied Shadrach, "friend
Piper. Again I say to thee, I will not pull off my
hat ; and, if necessary, I will depart with a flea in
mine ear, as thou art pleased to express thyself,
rather than give up the tenets of our faith."

" *Du galgen schivenkel,*" quoth the Heer ;-" does
thy religion lay in thy hat, that thou refusest to put
it off? But whether it does or not, I swear"—

Swear not all," cried the self-poised Shadrach.

"'Sblood ! but I will swear, and so shall Ludwig Varlett," cried the Heer ; whereupon Ludwig
hoisted the gates of his eloquence, and poured forth
such a torrent of expletives, that, had not Shadrach
been immoveable as his hat, he had been utterly
demolished. That invincible civil warrior, however, neither opened his eyes, nor altered his position, during all the hot fire of Counsellor Varlett,

but remained motionless, except the twirling of his thumbs.

"Friend Piper, is it thy pleasure to hear what I have got to say ? The spirit moveth me"—

"The spirit may move thee to the d—l," cried Peter, "or the flesh shall do it, if you don't pull off your hat, *du ans dem land gejacter kerl.*"

"Verily, I understand not thy jargon, friend Peter," rejoined Shadrach ; "neither will I go to him thou speakest of, at thine or any other man's bidding. Wilt thou hear the proposals of friend William Penn, or wilt thou not?"

"No, may I eat of the *teufel's braden* if I hear another word from that ugly mouth of thine, till you pull off your hat," exclaimed the choleric Heer, starting from his seat.

"Thou mayst eat what thou pleasest, friend Piper," rejoined the other; "and for my ugly mouth, since it offends thee, I will depart to whence I came." So saying, he leisurely turned himself round, and was proceeding on his way, when the Heer Piper, to whose choler the dry eloquence of Shadrach added fresh fuel, cried out, "Stop l" in a voice of thunder.

The machinery of Shadrach, which had been put in motion for his departure, stopped, accordingly, and he remained, standing in most rigid perpendicularity, with his back to the Heer, and his head turned over his shoulder, so as to meet his eye.

"I am stoppèd, friend Piper," quoth he.

, The Heer Piper, hereupon, directed Lob Dotterel, who was in attendance, as part of the puissance of the Governor of Elsingburgh, forthwith to procure him a hammer and a tenpenny nail, an order which that excellent and attentive officer obeyed with his usual alacrity.

"Art thou going to build thee an house, friend Piper, that thou callest for nails and hammers?" asked Shadrach.

"You shall see presently," answered the Heer. "Since your religion consists in wearing your hat, I shall take care you stick fast to the faith, by nailing it to your head, with this tenpenny nail."

"Thou mayst do as thou pleasest, friend Piper," replied Shadrach, unmoved by the threat. "We have endured worse than this, in the old world, and are ready for sufferance in the new. Even now, in yon eastern settlements, our brethren are expelled from the poor refuges they have sought, and chased, like beasts, from the haunts of the new-settled places, as if their blood was the blood of wolves, their hands the claws of tigers, and their feet the feet of the murderer. Our faith grew up in stripes, imprisonment, and sufferings, and behold, I am ready; smite—I am ready. The savage who hath no God, endures the tortures of fire, without shrinking, and shall not I dare to suffer, whom he sustains? Smite—I am ready."

The Heer was now in the predicament of certain passionate people, who threaten, what, when

it comes to the point, they shrink from inflicting.
Besides that the law of nations made the persons
of envoys sacred, he could not bring himself to
commit violence upon one, whose principles of non-
resistance were so inflexible.   By way of coming
off, therefore, with a good grace, he and Ludwig
Varlett fell into a great passion, and saluted Shadrach Moneypenny with a duet of expletives, which
that worthy plenipotentiary bore, for some· time,
with his usual stoical indifference.

    " Art thou ready, friend Piper," exclaimed ̄he,
taking advantage of the two singers being out of
breath. ·

    " Begone, and *der teufel hole dich*, and *das ton-
nerwetter schlage dich kreutzeveis in den boden*,"
cried the Heer.

    " I go, verily ;" and the good Shadrach marched
leisurely out of the council chamber, with his hands
crossed over his breast, his eyes turned upwards,
neither looking to the right nor to the left.   Coming
to the place where he had left his horse, he untied
him from the branch of an apple-tree, mounted by
the aid of a friendly rock, and seated himself in
the saddle; whereupon, he smote him in the side
with his unarmed heel, and the horse, taking the
hint, trotted off for the territory of Coaquanock.

    Thus was the negotiation between the powers
of Elsingburgh and Coaquanock, wrecked on a
point of etiquette, like that between England and
China, which happened in later times.   The obsti-

nacy of Shadrach, in not pulling off his hat to the Heer, and that of my Lord Amherst, in refusing to prostrate himself ever so many times before the elder brother of the moon, were both, in all probability, followed by consequences that affected millions of human beings, or will affect them at some future period. This proves the vast importance of etiquette, and we hope our worthy statesmen at the capital will persevere in their praiseworthy attempts, to make certain people, who don't know the importance of these matters, sensible of the absolute necessity of precedence being rigidly observed, in going into dining rooms, and sitting down to dinner.

CHAPTER VI.

What! shall not people pay for being govern'd?
Is't not the secret of the politic
To pigeon cits, and make the rogues believe
'Tis for the public good? By'r lady, sirs,
There shall not be a flea in an old rug,
Or bug in the most impenetrable hole
Of the bedstead, but shall pay
For the privilege of sucking Christian blood.
The Alderman; or, Beggars on Horseback.

WOLFGANG LANGFANGER, the long-headed member of the council of Elsingburgh, having, as we stated before, brought his private affairs into great confusion, by devoting too much of his time to the public good, began, a year or two before our history commences, to think it high time the public good should repay some part of its weighty obligations. He had accordingly invented, and persuaded the Heer Piper to put into practice, a system of internal improvement, which has been imitated, from time to time, in this country, ever since, with great success. The essence of his plan consisted in running in debt for the present, and living afterward upon the anticipation of future wealth.

It happened, about the time we refer to, that a schooner arrived from some part of New-England, with a cargo of odd notions, commanded by a

certain adventurer, who designated himself as
follows, to wit:—

> " Captain John Turner,
>   Master and owner
>   Of this cargo and schooner."

The sage Langfanger hailed this event as furnishing unquestionable augury that the town of Elsingburgh was destined to monopolize the commerce
of all the dominions of his Swedish majesty in the
new world, provided proper measures were taken
to improve its natural advantages. He accordingly
planned a great wharf, for the accommodation of
thirty or forty large ships, with stores for goods,
and every matter requisite for carrying on a great
trade.

Having provided for the external commerce of
Elsingburgh, Langfanger next turned his attention
to its internal trade, which consisted, as yet, in the
cargoes of a few bark canoes, in which the Indians
brought down muskrat and bear skins, to barter
for *tiger's milk*. In order to accommodate these,
he planned a canal, to connect the Brandywine
with the Delaware, by a cut, that would shorten
the distance at least six miles. By this he boasted
that the whole trade of the interior would centre
at Elsingburgh, to the complete abandonment and
destruction of Coaquanock, which must necessarily
dwindle into utter insignificance. ' The Heer was
excessively tickled with the idea of being so

effectually revenged upon Shadrach Moneypenny, and the rest of his old enemies, the Quakers.

His next project was that of beautifying the town, which, it must be confessed, was rather a rigmarole sort of place, built at random, the streets somewhat crooked, and the houses occasionally protruding themselves before their neighbours, in somewhat of an unmannerly manner. Langfanger proposed to revise the whole plan, widen many of the principal streets, lay out several others upon a magnificent scale, and pull down the houses that interfered with the improvement of the city, as he soon began to call the great town of Elsingburgh. The Heer was rather startled at this project, considering the expense of purchasing the houses to be pulled down, and the probable opposition of the good people who inhabited them. But Langfanger was never at a loss on these occasions.

He went forth among the villagers, with a string of arguments, deductions, calculations, and anticipations, enough to puzzle, if not convince, much wiser heads than those which grew on the shoulders of the simple inhabitants. Admitting only that his premises were true, and that what he predicted would certainly come to pass, and there was no denying his conclusions. Accordingly, the good people became assured that the pulling down their houses, and cutting up their gardens and fields into broad streets and avenues, would, in no little time, make every soul of them as rich as a Jew. It

was curious to see the apple trees cut down, the
grass cut up, and the lots carved into the most
whimsical shapes, by Wolfgang's improvements.

The beautiful grass-plots gave place to dusty or
muddy avenues, branching off in all directions,
and leading nowhere, insomuch that people could
hardly find their way anywhere. Houses, that
had hitherto fronted the street, now stood with
their backs to it, or presented a sharp corner ; and
the whole world was turned topsy-turvy at Elsingburgh. But the genius of Counsellor Langfanger
appeared to the greatest advantage in respect to
certain obstinate persons, who did not choose to
have their houses pulled down over their heads,
without being well paid for it. Wolfgang settled
matters with these, by causing the houses to be
valued at so much, and the improvement of the
property, in consequence of pulling them down, as
equivalent to the loss of the houses. These unreasonable persons were, by this equitable arrange-
ment, turned out of doors, and left to live very
comfortably upon the anticipation of a great rise
in the value of their estates.

Under the magnificent system of Counsellor
Wolfgang, the village of Elsingburgh grew and
flourished, by anticipation, beyond all former example ; although, since that time, many similar
wonders have been exhibited to the world. But
there are always drawbacks upon human prosperity—an inside, and an outside, to every thing.

The mischief was, that these great improvements
cost a great deal of money, and there was very
little of it to be had at Elsingburgh. Improvements
brought debts, and debts are as naturally followed
by taxes as a cow is by her tail. It became necessary, at least, to provide for the payment of the
interest upon the debt contracted, in consequence
of these invaluable improvements, in order to keep
up the public credit, and enable Counsellor Langfanger to carry on his schemes, and improve the
town, by running up a still heavier score. And
here we will take occasion to remark upon a great
singularity, which distinguishes the man who lays
out his own, from him who disburses the public
money. How careful is he, in the first instance,
to make the most of it, to turn every penny to his
advantage, and to weigh the probable gains in employing it before he parts with a dollar! Whereas,
on the contrary, when he hath the management
of the public funds, it is astonishing how liberal he
becomes; how his generosity expands, and upon
what questionable schemes he will expend millions
that do not belong to him. There is another pecu-
liarity, which ever accompanies the management
of the public wealth, which is, that let a man be
ever so honest beforehand, or ever so desirous to
exhibit to the world a pure example of disinterest-
edness, some of this money will stick to his fingers
in spite of his teeth, and bring his integrity into
question. This is doubtless the reason **why men**

are so unwilling to undertake these matters, and that only the warmest patriotism will induce them to have any thing to do with the public money.

But to return to our history. The worthy Counsellor Langfanger, by direction of Governor Piper, forthwith set about devising the ways and means to keep up public credit, and go on with the public improvements. Political economy, or the science of starving on philosophical principles, was not much understood at this time ; but genius supplies the want of precept and example. Counsellor Langfanger devised, and the Heer Piper adopted and enforced, a system of taxation more just and equally proportioned than any ever before known. Nobody was to be taxed above one per cent. on his property ; but then, the Heer reserved to himself to value the said property agreeably to his discretion. Accordingly, to make his revenues meet his improvements, he was obliged to rate lands at a sort of imaginary prospective value, at least three times greater than any body would give for them. The good people of Elsingburgh were highly astonished at finding themselves so rich, and paid their taxes cheerfully, until the perpetual drain upon their pockets, to meet Counsellor Langfanger's improvements, made it convenient to sell some part of their property, when they were utterly confounded to find themselves rich only according to the Heer Piper's tax list.

But agreeably to the homely old saying, "In for a

penny, in for a pound," Wolfgang assured them that if they stopped short in their improvements before they had got half through, all the money hitherto expended would be utterly lost; but if they only persevered to the end, they could not possibly fail of reaping a glorious harvest. The good folks scratched their heads, and paid their taxes. In the mean time the Heer and his counsellor every day discovered some new article to tax, until at length it came to pass, that every thing necessary to the existence of the people of Elsingburgh, every thing that belonged to them, to the very heads on their shoulders, and the coats on their backs, was loaded with imposts, to contribute to the great end of public improvement. It will be only anticipating the course of events a few years, to say that many of these projects of Counsellor Langfanger never realized the advantages he predicted, and of others that did, the profits were never reaped by those who paid for them, since a great portion of these were, in process of time, compelled to sell their property by piecemeal, to meet the perpetual exactions of the Heer Piper and his long-headed counsellor.

BOOK THIRD.

CHAPTER I.

Not to be meddled with except by philosophers.

If we examine, aided by the light of history, the course of human events, we shall find that every thing moves in a perpetual circle. The world turns round, and all things with it. Every thing new is only the revival of something forgotten; and what are called improvements, discoveries, or inventions, are, for the most part, little else than matters that have again come uppermost, by the eternal revolutions of the wheel of time. Mutability may be said to constitute the harmony of the universe, whose vast and apparent changes and varieties are produced, like those of music, by the same notes differently arranged.

" It is an ill wind that blows nobody good," says the old proverb, and accordingly we find, that causes which produce the misery of one being, bring about the happiness of another. The tear of one eye is balanced by the smile of another cheek; the agony of one heart, by the transports of another, originating in the same source. So, to extend our principle from individuals to nations,

the misfortunes of one contribute to the prosperity
of others; and, as the circle of events is completed, these very nations will be found to change
their relations with each other, the happy one being
wretched, the miserable one happy, in its turn.
It is thus, too, with the succeeding generations of
man. The struggles, violence, and crimes of a
revolution in one age, bring about a salutary re-
form of abuses, of which many generations reap
the benefits in future times ; and thus should every
suffering mortal solace himself with the comfortable assurance, that he is nothing more than a
martyr to the happiness of some unknown being,
who, in the course of events, will reap the harvest
in joy, of what hath been sown in tears.

Beyond doubt, many people who have not paid
proper attention to the absolute monotony which
characterizes the course of events in all ages of
the world, and which is produced by the revolutions of our wheel, are of opinion that those re-
finements in police, those schemes for public improvement, and that noble system of political
economy by which nations and communities are
enabled to get over head and ears in debt, are the
productions of the present age. But whoever
compares the system of the Heer Piper, and his
long-headed Counsellor Wolfgang Langfanger, with
that commonly in operation at this time in our
cities and states, will at once perceive it is nothing
more than the same thing brought up again in the

revolutions óf the great wheel, the *primum mobile* of human events. In detailing the various plans of Governor Piper, to make all, the little bad boys good by means of teaching them their A, B, C,; in his attempts to banish vice and poverty from Elsingburgh, by an ingenious mode of encouraging idleness; and in various other philanthropic schemes, which we shall from time to time develop, it will appear to demonstration, that he anticipated the present age by at least a century and a half. The evolutions of our wheel demonstrated their inutility in a few years; but the lessons of expericuce are ever forgotten when their effects cease to be felt, and another turn of the world brought these schemes uppermost again; whence they will again fall, after having given their impulse to the wheel, ás the water falls out of the buckets, runs away to put some other power in motion, or is exhaled in clouds, whence it falls in dews and showers, and once more replenishes the brook that turns the wheel.

CHAPTER II.

'It was reveal'd to Master SCRUPLE STRONG,
The pestilence last year did take its rise,
Not from foul air, but foul iniquities,
From wicked laughter in the public streets;
From teaching sinful parrots to swear oaths;
From wicked children spending all their pence
In luxuries of cakes and gingerbread;
But above all, from making sinful men,
Sheriffs, and such like dignitaries.
These loud crying sins did cause dry summers,
Make the sickness rage, and people die of fevers.
Balaam's Ass ; or, the Lecturer turned Hectorer.

THE Heer Piper, as we have seen in the preceding details, was principally influenced, in his
political designs, by the advice of Counsellor Langfanger; but he intrusted the administration of his
ecclesiastical affairs to Dominie Kanttwell, director
of the consciences of the good people of Elsingburgh. The Dominie, though a follower of Martin
Luther, had little of the liberality of that illustrious
reformer, being somewhat intolerant in his principles, bigoted in his doctrines, sour in his humour,
and a most bitter enemy to all sorts of innocent
sports, which he represented as the devil's toys,
with which that arch enemy seduced people from
their allegiance to the church. He held all the
surplus earnings of the poor, as well as all laying
up for the future, to be little better than a distrust-
ing of Providence; taking every opportunity to

assure his flock, that it was their duty to work hard all the week, shun all sorts of amusements and indulgences, and devote all they could earn to the good of the church, and the comfort of the parson. He pledged himself, if they would do this, they might be easy as to the wants of the future, since, in case of sickness, loss of crops, or any other accidents of life, some miraculous inter- position would never fail to take place, by which their wants would be supplied. Beans and bacon would rain down from heaven, partridges would fly in at their doors and windows, and all their wants would be administered to, as a reward for their generosity to the parson.

Dominie Kanttwell was a great dealer in judg- ments and miracles. The direct interposition of Providence was always visible to him, in every little accident that happened in the village; and while he preached that this world was a mere state of probation, a furnace where good men were tried by fire, and subjected to every species of suffering, he took every opportunity of contradicting this doctrine, by converting every little good or ill ac- cident that happened to his flock into a judgment or a miracle—a reward for going to church, and honouring the parson, or a punishment for neg- lecting both. On one occasion, the only child of a poor widow happened to be drowned in paddling a boat on the river, on the Sabbath morning. The Dominie immediately visited the afflicted parent, and comforted her with the assurance of its being a judgment upon her for not sending the boy to church. In the afternoon he thundered forth from the pulpit, and contrasted this unhappy catastrophe, or signal judgment of Providence, with the miracle of the poor man, who, notwithstanding he was over head and ears in debt, with a family of eight young children, had bestowed a part of his earnings upon a fund for converting the Hottentots, and was rewarded by a miraculous shot, by which he killed a fat buck, a thing he had never done before in all his life. What was very singular, however, and would have excited some little suspicion, in any other case but that of the Dominie, he never gave any thing away himself, or trusted to any of these miracles in his own particular case, it being a maxim of his, that to cause others to bestow their alms in charity, was equivalent to giving them himself. In short, he held the consoling and comfortable doctrine, that he was perfectly justified in indulging himself in the good things of this life, provided he could only persuade the poor of his flock to appropriate a portion of their necessary comforts to the great objects he had in view.

The principal of these objects was, to put a stop to all sinful recreations, such as dancing, singing wicked ballads about love and murder, indulging in the abominations of puppet shows, reading plays, poetry, and such heathen productions, and, in short, all those relaxations with which the cheerful and amiable feelings of our nature are so immediately connected. Hushed was the laugh, and mute the sprightly song, when Dominie Kanttwell went forth into the village ; and nothing was heard but the nasal twang of voices bellowing forth volumes of burning wrath, and eternal fires, to those who dared to be happy, in a moment of cessation from toil. These, together with certain tracts, containing wonderful accounts of conversions of young sinners of five years old, denunciations of eternal punishment upon wicked laughers, who dared to smile, even while the bottomless pit was yawning to receive them, together with pious exhortations to pay the Dominic well, and contribute to the conversion of the Hottentots, were the only relaxations and amusements permitted in the village of Elsingburgh.

Aided by the influence of the Heer, the eloquence of aunt Edith, and the activity of Lob Dotterel, the merry little village of Elsingburgh, in process of time, became a dull, torpid, dronish hive, where nothing was thought of but the bottomless pit. People neglected their labours to sing psalms, and instead of paying their debts, gave their money to the Dominie, trusting to a miracle for support in case of accident. Lob intruded himself into every house, in search of old ballads, and such like enormities, and never rested till he had succeeded, either by persuasion, threats, or bribery, in displacing these ancient memorials. These were replaced

by tracts, such as we have before specified, which
were printed on large sheets, to be pasted on the
walls, in the room of the carnal and wicked legends
of ballad poetry.

In a little while, there was not one of these to
be seen, except in the shop of a heterodox cobbler,
whose walls were decked with a numerous collection of old Swedish ballads, such as he had heard
in his youth ; and which were connected, and in-
tertwined with all the delightful recollections which
throng 'around the thoughts of our native home,
when we have left it for ever. These venerable
old legends were his choicest treasures, and con-
stituted the source of his principal delights. He
sung them while at work in his shop ; and in the
leisure of evenings sat at his door, chanting his
ditties in an agreeable voice, that never failed to
collect around him a crowd of little urchins, and
sometimes seduced the hearers from an opposite
house, where the Dominie and aunt Edith had instituted a society for celebrating the horrors of the
bottomless pit.

These seductions of the old ballads were highly
resented, and Lob Dotterel was directed to arm
himself with a quantity of tracts, replenish his paste
pot, and attack the ballads, tooth and nail. Crispin,
who had some idea that nobody had a right to
meddle with his ballads, resisted the high constable,
at first, with argument; but finding that Lob was
proceeding to displace his favourite ditty, very

discourteously seized him round the waist, threw
him out of the window, and emptied the paste-pot
upon Master Dotterel's head.   But this outrage of
the wicked cobbler was speedily punished, by a
special judgment, according to the theory of Dominic Kanttwell; who wisely employed human
means, however, to bring it about.   The Dominic
used all his influence, as well as that of the Heer
Piper and aunt Edith, to persuade people their shoes
would never prosper, if made, or even mended, by
the wicked, ballad-singing cobbler.   One, who
persisted, notwithstanding, in employing him, had
a new pair of shoes, made by poor Crispin, stolen
from him, the very night they were brought home,
by some heaven-inspired rogue.   The influence of
the Dominie, and his coadjutors, did not fail to bring
another judgment on the cobbler, who gradually
lost his custom, and with it, all heart to sing ballads.
The judgment was completed in a most singular
manner, by the destruction of his shop, ballads and
all, by a fire ; which, as nobody could tell how it
happened, was set down by the Dominie, in his next
Sunday's sermon, for a special interposition of
Providence.

The cobbler departed from the village, and
many years afterward, was discovered, as we shall
relate in the sequel, in the person of the wealthy
Burgomaster, or Alderman Spangler of New-York,
who had risen to wealth and city honours, and
loved old ballads as well as ever.   But this did not

impeach Dominic Kanttwell's miracle, or diminish
the confidence of the people of the village, in the
aptitude of Providence to revenge any offence to
that worthy person.   Honest Spangler, however,
died at a good old age, and directed the following
epitaph to be graven on his tomb stone, in proof
that he had preserved his respect for old ballads,
to the last:

> Here underneath this pair of stones,
> Rest honest Wolvert Spangler's bones,
> Who, in this city, prosper'd right well,
> Spite of the d—l and Dominie Kanttwell.
> He with his latest Christian breath,
> Bears testimony until death,
> That he never knew since he was born'd,
> An honest man that ballads scorn'd.

Wolvert was the last person that maintained the
legitimacy of old ballads in the village of Elsingburgh.   From the time of the signal judgment that
followed his contumacy, the sound of cheerful
gayety, the merry laugh, and sprightly dance were
no more heard or seen; and even the tinkling cow-
bell, that homely music whose simplicity so charm-
ingly accords with rural scenes and rural quiet,
was banished, because the wicked cows disturbed
the Dominie by tinkling them on Sabbath day.

The Dominic, and his zealous coadjutor aunt
Edith, rejoiced mightily in their work, and predicted wonderful effects from the downfall of wicked
ballads, profane singing, and the tinkling of the
cow-bells.   But it might be shrewdly observed,
that the corruptions of human nature are like those

of the blood, that break out into little pimples, which, though they disfigure the face somewhat, produce no fatal results, unless they are forcibly driven in, when they are apt to occasion the most mortal diseases. Physicians should be careful how they tamper with the pimples; and reformers should beware, lest, like unskilful tinkers, in stopping one hole, they open half a dozen others. It was thus with the result of Dominie Kanttwell's reforma-tions.

The worthy folks of Elsingburgh, being restrained in those little amusements and recreations, which, as it were, sanctify those hours of leisure, so dan-gerons to mankind in general, unless some license of this kind is allowed them, began to indulge in practices more fatal to the repose of society, and the happiness of mankind, than singing or dancing. The pimples disappeared from the surface, but the humours struck deeper within. The deep and dismal vices of gloom and superstition came in the place of cheerful amusements; and it was ob-served, that more instances of overreaching in bargains, more interruptions in social harmony, and more lapses from chastity, took place in one year, than formerly occurred in five. The ignorant seemed to think they obtained a license for certain worldly offences, by practising the outward forms of piety, and giving money to the Dominie; while the evil disposed made religion a cloak for their hypocrisy.

But these were not the only consequences of this system of coaxing the poor out of the surplus of their little earnings, for pious purposes, and trusting to miracles in time of need, backed by the proscription of smiles and song. Instead of laying up something for rainy days, and providing against those ebbs of fortune which occur so frequently in the tide of human affairs, they parted with these little nest-eggs, trusting to the assurances of Dominie Kanttwell, that if the worst came to the worst, they would be fed like the prophet, even by the ravens. But when these trying seasons came, when the mildew spoiled the harvest, or sickness unnerved the arm of the lusty tradesman, it often came to pass, that the bitter effects of neglecting worldly means fell heavily upon them. The partridge did not fly in at the window, nor the unskilful marksman always hit his deer. Poverty, the inevitable consequence of relying on miracles for relief, at least in these latter days, came to be the portion of many.

To meet these visitations, the Dominie, with the aid of aunt Edith, instituted a society for the relief of these unfortunate people, thus suffering for their faith in miracles. Those who chanced to have preserved that little surplus, so essential to the welfare of the labouring classes, were induced to part with a portion of it, and thus to prepare themselves for becoming objects of charity in turn, by placing their future wants at the mercy of the rubs

and accidents of life. Those who found it more
agreeable to live without labour, at the expense of
others, seeing they could now indulge their wishes,
without suffering the consequences of idleness,
gradually remitted their labours, both of earning
and saving. Thus recruits poured in on every
side; idleness increased; extravagance spread
abroad; and, in no long period of time, the little
industrious community of Elsingburgh, where a
beggar had hitherto never been seen, became a
nest of paupers. The busy Dominie, together with
his zealous assistant, then set about instituting societies of other kinds, for the relief of these growing
miseries. But the more societies they formed, the
more beggary and idleness increased. Counsellor
Langfanger was then consulted, as to the best
remedy for these crying evils; and accordingly,
advised a society for the encouragement of industry.
But this plan unluckily failed, owing to the extraordinary fact, that so long as the other societies
offered relief without working, nobody applied for
employment, to the society for encouraging industry. So easy is it to make people worse, in
trying to make them better!

CHAPTER III.

There was a madman, mad as a March hare could be,
And people swore that no man could madder be than he ;
But the madman was resolved, even with them to be,
So he swore that all the world was mad, excepting only he.

Our youthful readers may perhaps be inclined to suspect that we have forgotten our heroine, and lost sight of the principal object of every history of this kind, which ought always to be that of throwing as many obstacles in the way of the happiness of lovers as possible. But the suspicion is entirely groundless. The fair Christina is not an object to be so easily overlooked ; and though we may occasionally turn aside from her affairs, to graver matters of state, it is only with a view of giving our lovers an opportunity of enjoying, without interruption, those innocent, and never-to-be-forgotten delights, that accompany the early dawnings of affection ; and to which the aged always look back as the happiest period of existence.

The blue-eyed maid, and the fair tall youth, were left pretty much to themselves, during the progress of the autumnal season, the governor and aunt Edith being both, as we have before stated, busily employed, the one in public improvements, the other reforming mankind. The youthful pair sung, and read, and rambled together ; and every passing day added to the strength of those ties, which were gradually uniting their hearts for ever. Koningsmarke, although his actions and looks expressed all the feelings of a devoted attachment, never made any explicit declaration on the subject, for both seemed satisfied with the sweet consciousness of mutual attachment. Christina had no rivals in the village, and Othman Pfegel treated her with a sort of pouting indifference, seldom intruding on their lonely rambles, or disturbing their domestic enjoyments.

But Christina was far from being happy. She could not deceive herself with the hope, that her affection would be sanctioned by her father's approbation; and every new feeling that developed itself in the progress of her affections, served to convince her that a time would come, when a more intimate union would be necessary to her happiness. Besides this, certain indefinable and vague suspicions, which, ever as she chased them from her mind, returned again to haunt her lonely. musings, gave her many a heartache. These suspicions were kept alive by the sudden and unaccountable changes in the expression of Koningsmarke's eye, which occasionally indicated a wild ferocity, as well as by the mysterious warnings of the Snow Ball, who took every opportunity of uttering most fearful oracles, that Christina could not comprehend, but which excited vague apprehensions.

She became gradually fond of solitude, and often

indulged herself in long and lonely walks, usually following the course of the little stream, whose windings led to the forests, which spread their endless shades towards the west, the haunt of Indians and their game.

These neighbouring Indians were, for the most part, on friendly terms with the whites at Elsingburgh; but occasionally, took little miffs, and committed depredations on the cattle and fields.

On the banks of this stream, about a mile, or perhaps a mile and a half from the village, resided a singular being ; a white man, who came there about fifteen years from the period of which we are treating, and had ever since lived alone on that spot. His dwelling consisted of dry sticks, supported on one side by an old log, on the other by the earth, and covered over with leaves. It was neither sufficiently high to allow him to stand upright, nor long enough to permit him to lie at full length. He possessed no means for lighting or preserving fire, but, in the coldest weather, contented himself with crawling into his hut, stopping the mouth of it with leaves, and remaining there till hunger drove him forth. Yet he appeared to delight in this miserable mode of existence, which no persuasion could induce him to forsake, to join in participating in the labours and enjoyments of social life. He enjoyed perfect health, and never asked charity, except when neither nuts nor apples could be procured in the woods and orchards. Then he would appear in the village, uttering certain unintelligible sounds, which the people understood as expressive of his wants, and relieved him accordingly. For fifteen years this solitary being had never been heard to speak a single word that could be understood, either from a natural dumbness, a derangement of mind, or a wish to escape all questioning, as to who he was, or whence he came, two things that nobody ever knew. He seemed, however, a harmless being, and when the people got a little used to him, he ceased to excite either curiosity or apprehension.

Christina often walked that way, without thinking of the hermit, or fearing any outrage; although there had been rumours in the village, that he was once or twice seen, about the full of the moon, in a paroxysm of raving insanity.

One afternoon she stole away from Koningsmarke, to take a solitary walk along the brook-side, and strolled as far as the hut, which happening to be untenanted at that moment, she sat down near to it on the bank of the stream. It chanced that a little popular song of her own country, which turns on a breach of constancy on the part of a young woman, came over her mind, and she was humming it to herself, when a wild and horrible laugh alarmed her fears. She started up, and looking round, beheld the hermit, coming towards her with the look and action of a maniac.

" Ha ! ha !" he exclaimed ; " have I found you

at last, faithless, inconstant girl! Thou art she—
I know thee by thy song."

Thus saying, he rushed towards the affrighted
maid, and attempted to drag her towards his hut.
Christina struggled, and begged him for God's sake
to release her; but his violence only increased
with opposition. His eyes flashed fire, he gnashed
his teeth; and foamed at the mouth in horrible
ecstacy.

"O! for pity's sake—for the sake of Heaven, my
father, all those who have been kind to you, let me
go—I am not her you think; my name is Christina."

"False, deceitful woman," cried the maniac;
"did I not hear thee sing the song—the very song!
do I not know thee by thy soft blue eye, thy curling
flaxy hair, thy voice, thy very breath, whose sweet-
ness I once used to inhale? Thou hast sought me,
to laugh at my misery and triumph in my wrongs.
But come—come in," added he in a hurried tone—
"come in; the bridal bed is made; I have waited
for you many long wintry nights, when the wolves
howled, and thought you'd never come. In—in
—we shall be happy yet."

So saying, he again attempted to force her
towards the door of his wretched hut. The poor
girl shrieked and struggled with all her might, and
the fury of the madman increased with her resistance. He dragged her forcibly along, and when
she caught by the young trees, to enable her to
resist more effectually, cruelly bruised her tender

hands, to force her to let go her hold.   Gradually
her powers of resistance gave way to a fainting,
deadly languor.   Again she shrieked; and at that
moment a man with a gun darted from the woods
towards them.   The maniac let go his hold, and,
ere the stranger could point his gun, darted forward and seized it with both hands.   A mortal
struggle ensued.   The maniac, with a desperate
effort, snatched the gun from the other; who,
springing forward, seized him round the waist, and
forced him to drop the weapon in order to defend
himself.   They fell, the stranger uppermost; but
in the act of falling, the maniac seized him by his
ruff, tore it off, grappled his neck with his long
nails, and, burying his teeth in his flesh, seemed to
enjoy the sucking of his blood.   Koningsmarke, for
it was he, turned black in the face, and his eyes
became gradually almost shrouded in darkness,
when, with a convulsive effort, he placed his knee
on the breast of the maniac, drew himself up on a
sudden, and loosed his hold.   Both started up; but
Koningsmarke had a moment's advantage, which
he employed in seizing the gun and running a few
steps from him.   The other followed.

"Stand off," cried Koningsmarke.   "Were I
alone, I would give you a fair chance; but the
life and happiness of an angel is at stake.   Stand
off—or—"

The maniac advanced—one—two steps. The
third was the step to eternity.   The piece went

off with a true aim; he uttered a yelling laugh,
jumped into the air, and fell without sense or motion.   Koningsmarke, after satisfying himself that
all was over with the poor wretch, hastened to
Christina, who was lying insensible, with her hair
dishevelled, her garments torn, and her cheeks as
white as the pure and snowy bosom, whose modest
covering had been displaced in the struggle.   He
called her his dear Christina ; he ran to the brook
for water to sprinkle her face; and kissed the
drops as they rolled down her pale cheeks.   At
length she opened her eyes, gazed for a moment
as if bewildered, and shut them again.   By degrees,
however, she recovered a recollection of her situation—adjusted her dress, and essayed to express
her gratitude.   But her voice failed her.   She saw
the blood running from the neck of her deliverer,
wiped it away with her hair, and wistfully gazing
on the wound, cried out with an expression of horrible and sudden despair—" The scar ! the scar !"
Covering her face with both her hands, she groaned
in the agony of conflicting emotions, and throwing
herself to the earth, was relieved from distraction
by a shower of tears.

It was now evening—the youth raised her up,
placed her arm within his, and pressed it tenderly
to his heart.   Christina shuddered, and looked up
in his face with an expression so tender, yet so
wretched, that had not his conscious heart told him
it was now impossible, he would have asked her to

be his for ever. They walked home without uttering a word, and were received with a very bad
grace by the Heer, who did not much like their
walking so late by moon-light. But when he heard
the story of Christina's deliverance from the blue-
eyed maiden herself, he wept over her like an
infant, and, grasping the Long Finne in his arms,
blessed the youth, and called him his dear son.

A long illness followed this adventure, on the
part of Christina, and when her health was apparently restored, her innocent sprightliness, her
buoyant step, rosy cheek, laughing eye, and all
the bright hopes which youth delights to cherish,
seemed gone for ever. From this time forward, the
character and deportment of the poor girl seemed
to have undergone a great change. Violent bursts
of gayety, followed by instantaneous gloom and
despondency; laughter and tears; listless acquiescence, or obstinate opposition to the wishes of
all around her, bespoke either an unsettled mind,
or a heart torn by contending feelings. It was
believed that the fright of her late adventure had
unsettled her nerves, and all the wise old women
of the village prescribed for her in vain.

But her deportment towards the Long Finne was
marked by the most sudden and extraordinary
inconsistencies. Sometimes she would silently
contemplate his face, till the tears gushed from
her eyes; and at others, when he came suddenly
into her presence, utter a scream of agonized feel-

ing, and flee from his presence with a look of horror. She would sometimes consent to take the
arm of the youth, and walk along the river side,
and then, as if from a sudden and irresistible impulse, snatch it away, and recoil from him, as from
the touch of a serpent. In short, every passing
day made it more and more apparent, that she was
struggling with powerful and contending emotions,
that obtained an alternate mastery, and governed
her actions, for the moment, with unlimited sway.

Koningsmarke, though he saw, and appeared to
lament this change in her character, never essayed
to draw from her the cause. He seemed deterred
by a secret consciousness, that a full explanation
would do him at least no good, and continued his
attentions as usual.

Bombie of the Frizzled Head acted a conspicu-
ous part at this time, and became more incomprehensible than ever. She seemed to know the secret
of all these wonders, but would tell nothing of what
she knew; contenting herself with a more than
usual quantity of mysterious warnings, too well
now understood by Christina, but incomprehensible
to her father. The Heer often cursed her in the
bitterness of his perplexity, exclaiming—"why dost
thou not speak out, thou execrable Snow Ball."
But Bombie only shook her head, and replied as
usual: "I have seen what I have seen—I know
what I know."

One day as Koningsmarke had taken a solitary

walk, and was seated on the bank of the stream, close by the hut of the solitary stranger, reflecting painfully on matters that deeply concerned himself, he was roused from his reverie by the well-known voice of the Snow Ball, calling out "Koningsmarke l"

᠂ " I am here," he replied.

" Thou art here, when thou shouldst be far away," cried the Snow Ball. "Art thou not satisfied with the mother's fate, that thou hungerest for the ruin of the daughter's happiness? Go thy ways, or I will tell what I have seen, and what I know."

"Who will believe thee?" replied the Long Finne. " Thou art a slave, and canst not witness against him that is free. I have been long enough a wanderer, without a resting place; I have found a home at last, and I will not go hence. Tell what thou wilt; I care not."

"Ay,". cried the sibyl, " thou hast found a home, at the price of misery to those who afford thee a shelter; thou hast turned viper, and stung him that warmed thee at his fire ; thou hast nestled thyself into an innocent bosom, to destroy its repose, or corrupt its innocence, and tortured the heart that would, ay, and will yet, die for thee, if thou lingerest here. Depart, I say, and let this one act towards the daughter atone 'for thine acts to the mother."

The Long Finne wrung his hands, and the tears

rolled down his cheeks, as he exclaimed, "Woman! woman! whither shall I go? I would remain here, where none but thou and ⸺ know who I am, and atone for the past, by devoting myself to the happiness of Christina and her father. This is my only chance; for if I go hence an outcast, I shall become—what I once was. The fate of mine immortal soul turns upon this cast."

"It is too late," replied the other; "SHE KNOWS IT NOW. Dost thou not see it in her tears, her struggles, her pale cheek, and wild and hollow eyes? It is too late; if thou stayest she dies—if thou goest speedily, she may yet live. Hence, then, and never let her see thee more."

"Away, old raven," answered the youth, resuming his obduracy. "If SHE should rise from the dead, and motion me with her fleshless finger, to the north or the south, the east or the west—nay, if I saw the hand of fate pointing to the destruction of myself and all around me, I would stay."

The sibyl dropped her horn-headed cane, raised her bent, decrepit figure, till she stood upright as the tall pine, threw her hands and eyes towards heaven, and cried out, in the bitterness of her heart—

"Stay then—and may the curse of the wicked come swiftly upon thee. May the sorrows thou hast caused unto others recoil tenfold upon thy blasted head. May the malediction of the father, who opened his house to thee, crush the spoiler.

May the forgiveness of her who will die forgiving thee, be but the forerunner of thine eternal condemnation to that fire which is never quenched and never consumes."

Again Bombie relapsed into her usual stooping attitude, picked up her stick, and disappeared, leaving the youth with a load of consciousness on his heart, but with a determined purpose not to depart from Elsingburgh.

CHAPTER IV.

"Cold and raw the north winds blow,
Bleak in the morning early;
All the hills are covered with snow,
And winter's now come fairly."

WINTER, with silver locks and sparkling icicles, now gradually approached, under cover of his north-west winds, his pelting storms, cold, frosty mornings, and bitter, freezing nights. And here we will take occasion to express our obligations to the popular author of the PIONEERS, for the pleasure we have derived from his happy delineations of the progress of our seasons, and the successive changes which mark their course. All that remember their youthful days in the country, and look back with tender, melancholy enjoyment, upon their slippery gambols on the ice, their Christmas pies, and nut-crackings by the cheerful fireside, will read his pages with a gratified spirit, and thank him heartily for having refreshed their memory, with the half-effaced recollections of scenes and manners, labours and delights, which, in the progress of time, and the changes which every where mark his course, will in some future age, perhaps, live only in the touches of his pen. If, in the course of our history, we should chance to dwell upon scenes somewhat similar to those he describes, or to mark the varying tints of our seasons, with a sameness of colouring, let us not be stigmatized with borrowing from him, since we only copy from the same original.

The holydays, those wintry blessings, which cheer the heart of young and old, and give to the gloomy depths of winter the life and spirit of laughing, jolly spring, were now near at hand. The chopping-knife gave token of goodly minced pies, and the bustle of the kitchen afforded shrewd indications of what was coming by and by. The celebration of the new year, it is well known, came originally from the northern nations of Europe, who still keep up many of the practices, amusements, and enjoyments, known to their ancestors. The Heer Piper valued himself upon being a genuine northern man, and consequently, held the winter holydays in special favour and affection. In addition to this hereditary attachment to ancient customs, it was shrewdly suspected, that his zeal in celebrating these good old sports was not a little quickened, in consequence of his mortal antagonist, William Penn, having hinted, in the course of their controversy, that the practice of keeping holydays savoured not only of popery, but paganism.

Before the Heer consented to sanction the projects of Dominie Kanttwell for abolishing sports and ballads, he stipulated for full liberty, on the part of himself and his people of Elsingburgh, to eat, drink, sing and frolic as much as they liked, during the winter holydays.   In fact, the Dominie made no particular opposition to this suspension of his blue laws, being somewhat addicted to good eating and drinking, whenever the occasion justified ; that is to say, whenever such accidents came in his way.

It had long been the custom with Governor Piper, to usher in the new year with a grand supper, to which the Dominie, the members of the council, and certain of the most respectable burghers, were always bidden. This year, he determined to see the old year out, and the new one in, as the phrase was, having just heard of a great victory gained by the bulwark of the Protestant religion, the immortal Gustavus Adolphus ; which, though it happened nearly four years before, had only now reached the village of Elsingburgh.   Accordingly, the Snow Ball Bombie was set to work in the cooking of a mortal supper ; which, agreeably to the taste of West Indian epicures, she seasoned with such enormous quantities of red pepper, that whoever ate, was obliged to drink, to keep his mouth from getting on fire, like unto a chimney.

Exactly at ten o'clock, the guests sat down to the table, where they ate and drank to the success of the Protestant cause, the glory of the great Gustavus, the downfall of Popery and the Quakers, with equal zeal and patriotism.   The instant the clock struck twelve, a round was fired from the fort, and a vast and bottomless bowl, supposed to be the identical one in which the famous wise men of Gotham went to sea, was brought in, filled to the utmost brim with smoking punch. The memory of the departed year, and the hopes of the future, was then drank in a special bumper, after which the ladies retired, and noise and fun became the order of the night. The Heer told his great story of having surprised and taken a whole picquet-guard, under the great Gustavus ; and each of the guests contributed his tale, taking special care, however, not to outdo their host in the marvellous, a thing which always put the governor out of humour.

Counsellor Langfanger talked wonderfully about public improvements ; Counsellor Varlett sung, or rather roared, a hundred verses of a song in praise of Rhenish wine ; and Othman Pfegel smoked and tippled, till he actually came to a determination of bringing matters to a crisis with the fair Christina the very next day. Such are the wonder-working powers of hot punch! As for the Dominie, he departed about the dawn of day, m such a plight, that if it had not been impossible, we should have suspected him of being, as it were, a little overtaken with the said punch. To one or two persons who chanced to see him, he actually appeared to stagger a little ; but such was the stout faith of the good Dominie's parishioners, that neither of these worthy fellows would believe his own eyes sufficiently to state these particulars.

A couple of hours sleep sufficed to disperse the
vapours of punch and pepper-pot; for heads in
those days were much harder than now, and the
Heer, as well as his roistering companions, rose
betimes to give and receive the compliments and
good wishes of the season. The morning was
still, clear, and frosty. The sun shone with the
lustre, though not with the warmth of summer,
and his bright beams were reflected with indescribable splendour, from the glassy, smooth ex-
panse of ice, that spread across, and up and down
the broad river, far as the eye could see. The
smoke of the village chimneys rose straight into
the air, looking like so many inverted pyramids,
spreading gradually broader, and broader, until
they melted away, and mixed imperceptibly with
ether. Scarce was the sun above the horizon,
when the village was alive with rosy boys and girls,
dressed in their new suits, and going forth with such
warm anticipations of happiness, as time and experience imperceptibly fritter away, into languid
hopes, or strengthening apprehensions. "Happy
New Year!" came from every mouth, and every
heart. Spiced beverages and lusty cakes, were
given away with liberal open hand; every body
was welcomed to every house; all seemed to
forget their little heart-burnings, and disputes of
yore—all seemed happy, and all were so; and
the Dominie, who always wore his coat with four
great pockets on new-year's day, came home and

emptied them seven times, of loads of new-year cookies.

When the gay groups had finished their rounds in the village, the ice in front was seen all alive with the small fry of Elsingburgh, gambolling and skating, sliding and tumbling, helter skelter, and making the frost-bit ears of winter glad with the sounds of mirth and revelry. In one place was a group playing at hurley, with crooked sticks, with which they sometimes hit the ball, and sometimes each other's shins. In another a knot of sliders, following in a row, so that if the foremost fell, the rest were sure to tumble over him. A little farther might be seen a few, that had the good fortune to possess a pair of skates, luxuriating in that most graceful of all exercises, and emulated by some half a dozen little urchins, with smooth bones fastened to their feet, in imitation of the others, skating away with a gravity and perseverance worthy of better implements. All was rout, laughter, revelry, and happiness; and that day the icy mirror of the noble Delaware reflected as light hearts as ever beat together in the new world. At twelve o'clock, the jolly Heer, according to his immemorial custom, went forth from the edge of the river, distributing apples, and other dainties, together with handsful of wampum, which, rolling away on the ice in different directions, occasioned innumerable contests and squabbles among the fry, whose disputes, tumbles, and occasional buffetings for the prizes,

were inimitably ludicrous upon the slippery element. Among the most obstreperous and mischievous of the crowd was that likely fellow Cupid,
who made more noise, and tripped up more heels
that day, than any half a dozen of his cotempora-
ries. His voice could be heard above all the rest,
especially after the arrival of the Heer, before
whom he seemed to think it his duty to exert himself, while his unrestrained, extravagant laugh,
exhibited that singular hilarity of spirit which distinguishes the deportment of the African slave from
the invariable gravity of the free red man of the
western world.

All day, and until after the sun had set and the
shadows of night succeeded, the sports continued,
and the merry sounds rung far and near, occasionally interrupted by those loud noises, which
sometimes shoot across the ice like a rushing earth-
quake, and are occasioned by its cracking, as the
water rises or falls. All at once, however, these
bursts of noisy merriment ceased, and were succeeded by a hollow, indistinct murmur, which gradually died away, giving place to a single voice,
calling, as if from a distance, with a voice growing
feebler at every repetition, "Help!—help!—help!"

Presently it was rumoured, that a traveller,
coming down the river on the ice, had fallen into
what is called an air-hole, occasioned by the tide,
which was stronger at this spot, in consequence of
the jutting out of a low, rocky point. In places of

this sort, the ice does not cease all at once, but becomes gradually thinner and weaker towards the centre, where there is an open, unfrozen space. The consequence is, that if a person happens to be so unfortunate as to fall into one of these places, which are, in fact, hardly distinguishable at night from the solid ice, it is next to impossible to escape by his own efforts, or to be relieved by those of others. As fast as he raises himself upon the ice, it breaks from under him, and every effort diminishes his strength, without affording him relief. Thus the poor wretch continues his hopeless struggles, and becomes gradually weaker and weaker, until, finally, his blood is chilled, his limbs become inflexible, he loses his hold, and sinks to rise no more.

The same cause that forbids his relieving himself, operates in preventing others; since, if any one were to approach sufficiently near to reach his hand, the ice would break under him, and both would perish together. In this situation was the poor man whose cries were now heard, at intervals, growing weaker and weaker. All the village was out, and many hardy spirits, actuated by feelings of humanity, made vain and desperate attempts to approach sufficiently near to afford assistance. But although several risked their lives, none succeeded; and at length the conviction that his fate was inevitable, was announced in a dismal groan from the by-standers. At this moment the Long Finne approached, with two boards upon his

shoulder, which he brought as near to the opening
as was safe to approach. Standing exactly at this
line, he threw one of the boards upon the ice before him, and, dragging the other after, proceeded
cautiously along to the end. Then he drew up
the other board and threw it before him, walking
steadily and cautiously on that, dragging the other
after him as before. In this manner, while the
by-standers watched in breathless silence, he gradually approached the opening, encouraging the poor
man to hold out, for God's sake, a few moments
longer.

. At last he came near enough to throw him a
cord, which he had brought with him. The perishing wretch caught it, and while Koningsmarke
held the other end, essayed to raise himself out
of the water by its assistance. But the effort was
beyond his strength, the ice again broke under him,
and he disappeared, as all thought, for ever. He
arose, however, with a desperate effort. " Tie the
cord around your waist," cried the youth. " My
fingers are stiff with cold," replied the other, "and
if I let go the ice, I am gone." Koningsmarke
now crawled on his hand and knees on one of the
boards, and pushing the other before him, cautiously crept to the end of the advanced board.
He was near enough to reach the hand of the
drowning man, and to fasten the cord about his
arm. Then receding in the manner he had advanced, he threw the other end of the cord to the

people, who dragged the poor wretch out of the water, with a shout that announced the triumph of courage and humanity.

During the whole of the scene we have just described, the anxiety of Christina had been excited in the most painful manner. At first, the situation of the poor perishing traveller monopolized her feelings; but when it was told her, that the Long Finne was risking his life for the stranger, her apprehensions rose to agony; she wrung her hands, and, unconscious of the presence of any body, would exclaim, " he will be drowned, he will be drowned !" The hollow voice of the Frizzled Head answered, and said, " be not afraid; the race of him for whose safety thou fearest, is not destined to close here. He will not perish by water."

" What meanest thou !" exclaimed the apprehensive girl.

" He will go upwards, not downwards, out of the world," replied the Frizzled Head, and glided out of the room.

Now was heard the noise of many footsteps, and many tongues, approaching, and Christina summoned her fortitude to go down stairs, for the purpose of offering her assistance, should it be necessary. The body of the stranger, now almost stiff and frozen, was brought in, laid in a bed with warm blankets, and every means taken to restore the waning circulation. Slowly, these applications had the desired effect: the stranger gradually re-

covered. He announced himself as from Coaquanock, and as being on his way down to the Hoar
Kill, having taken the ice, as the best and most
direct path thither. The worthy Heer, whose
generous feelings never failed to conquer his antipathies, treated the stranger with the greatest
kindness, during his progress to a perfect recovery;
praised and caressed the Long Finne, for his gallant presence of mind; and finally observed, " I
would give twenty rix-dollars, if the *galgen schivenkel* had been any thing save a Quaker.

CHAPTER V.

Bonny lass! bonny lass! will you be mine?
Thou shalt neither wash dishes, nor serve the wine?
But sit on a cushion, and sew up a seam,
And dine upon strawberries, sugar and cream."
Mother Goose's Melodies.

FORTUNE, or fate, or call it what you will, seemed to have ordained that the struggles of the fair Christina, between filial piety and youthful love, should be perpetually revived, and become more painfully bitter by the conduct of the Long Finne. He had saved her from the violence of the maniac, and thus excited her everlasting gratitude; and soon after performed an act of daring humanity, that called forth all her admiration. Thus every effort she made to drive him from her heart, was met by some action of his, that only riveted him more strongly there.

Gradually, during the long winter, she withdrew herself as much as possible from the society of the youth, and avoided all private interviews, or solitary walks. She was one of those rare females, the rarest and the most valuable of all the blessed race of women, who never suffer the weakness of their nerves, or the intensity of their feelings, to interfere with filial, maternal, or domestic duties. She was aware that this was little else than the indul-

gence of an overwrought self-love, and that employment in the discharge of one's duties, is twice
blessed—blessed in the happiness it communicates
to those within the sphere of its influence, and
blessed in the balm it administers to our own sorrows. She became even more unremitting than
ever, in attending upon her father, administering
to his little infirmities, and anticipating all his wants.
She never willingly subjected herself to the dangers of idleness, but sought, on all occasions, to
force her mind from painful contemplation, by the
performance of her domestic duties. Still there
were long hours of the night, when she could not
be busy, and when, in silence and solitude, her
woes clustered around her like shadowy demons,
destroying the blessed comfort of a quiet sleep, by
awakening recollections of the past unaccompanied
by pleasure, and anticipations of the future desti-
tute of hope. The paleness of her cheek, the languor of her figure, and her eye, gradually became
more and more apparent, until at last the good
Heer began to observe, and to be alarmed at her
looks.

In the mean time, the Long Finne passed whole
days in the woods, with his dog and gun, either to
relieve Christina from his presence, or to hide his
own feelings in the depths of the forest, where the
axe of the woodman, or the voice of a civilized
being, had never been heard. Sometimes he
crossed the river on the ice, and penetrated into

the pines, which reared their green heads into the heavens, and presented, in their dark foliage, a contrast to the white snow, that, if possible, added to the wintry gloom. At other times, he turned his steps westward, where, save a little cultivated space about the village, one vast and uninterrupted world of forest tended, as it were, to the regions of the setting sun. Here he roamed about, immersed in thoughts as gloomy as the black wintry woods over his head, and unconscious of his purpose, until the whirring partridge, suddenly rising and thundering among the branches, or the barking of his dog at a squirrel, or occasionally at a bear, roused his attention. He seldom brought home any game, and numerous were the jests which the Heer cracked on his want of skill in the noble sports of hunting. The Long Finne would often have been lost in the woods, had it not been for his dog, who, with unerring sagacity, always showed him the way home.

One day, we believe it might have been towards the latter end of February, Koningsmarke set forth on his customary ramble, with his gun on his shoulder, his tinder-box, flint, and steel, the indispensable appendages in those pathless woods. He whistled, and called for his dog, but the animal had been seduced away, in the pure spirit of mischief, by that likely fellow, Cupid. Koningsmarke, therefore, proceeded without him, with a friendly caution from the Heer, to look which way he went,

not to wander too far, and, with an arch wink, to
be sure and bring home a fat haunch of venison.,
The Long Finne soon forgot the advice, and the
joke, and before noon, had wandered so far into
the forest,. that he could see none of his usual
landmarks, nor any object which he recognised.
Towards one o'clock it became overcast, raw and
chilly, and every thing presaged a storm.   The
youth thought it high time to retrace his steps ; but
without some path, or some guide, to direct his
course, a man in a great forest only walks in a
circle.   He heard that dreary, dismal howl, which
is caused by the wind rushing among the leafless
branches of the trees, gradually increase, and
swell, and sharpen, till it became a shrill whistle
that made his blood run cold.   In a little time the
snow began to fall in almost imperceptible parti-
cles, indicating not only intense cold, but a long-
continued and heavy,storm.   The Long Finne had
just made a discovery that he had lost his way,
and that if he did not speedily find it, the chances
were ten to one, that he perished that night in the
snow.   Now, though he had, in the course of his
day's·ramble, twice come to a resolution to put an
end to his miserable perplexities by shooting himself through the head, he felt not a little startled at
the dangers of his present situation.   There is a
great difference between a man dying of his own
accord, and dying because he cannot help it.   The
one is an act of free will, whereas the other smacks

of coercion; and men no more like to die, than
Jack Falstaff did to'give a reason, upon compulsion.

Our hero, accordingly, tacitly agreed with himself to postpone dying for the present, and make
use of the few remaining hours of daylight to seek
his way home.   But in his perplexity, he wandered
about in the labyrinths of the forest until near dark,
without recognising any object that could assist in
deciding where he was.   He hallooed, and fancied
he heard the barking of a dog, but when he approached it nearer, it turned out to be the howling
of a wolf.   At another time he heard, afar off, the
long echoes of a gun, but, in the depths of the
woods, could not distinguish the direction in which
it was fired.

The dusky shadows of night began to gather
around, and reminded him that if darkness over-
took him before he had prepared some kind of
shelter, he would never see the morning.   In looking about, he observed a large pine tree that had
been blown down, to the roots of which was attached a quantity of earth, which afforded some
shelter in that quarter.   The snow had drifted
against the windward side of the fallen trunk, and,
as frequently happens, left a bare space on the
leeward.   By scraping under the snow, he gathered a quantity of dry leaves, with which he made
a bed ; and contrived a sort of covering, by breaking off the branches of the fallen pine, and laying
them with one end on the ground, the other resting

on the trunk of the tree. He then collected a
quantity of brush, dry wood, and leaves, with which
to keep fire during the night, for such was the' intensity of the cold, that without the aid of artificial
warmth, he must have inevitably perished before
morning. By the time these preparations were finished it was quite dark; the wind whistled louder and
louder through the leafless branches, that cracked
in the onset, and the storm every moment increased
in violence.

In painful anxiety the Long Finne prepared his
implements for striking fire, and collected some of
the driest leaves and sticks, for the purpose of
lighting them with his tinder. In his eagerness to
strike fire, the flint flew from his benumbed hand,
and he could not find it again in the obscurity that
surrounded him. He then unscrewed the flint
from his gun; but, just at the instant the sparks
had communicated to the tinder, a sudden puff of
wind blew it out of the box, and scattered it in the
air. A moment of irresolution and despair, and
he bethought himself of one more chance for his
life. He replaced the flint in his gun, which he
fired off against the trunk of the fallen tree; the
burning wad fell upon the dry leaves placed there,
and by carefully blowing it with his mouth, a little
flame was produced, which at length caught the
leaves, and relieved his breathless anxiety. ·

He carefully placed the wood over the leaves,
until a blazing fire illuminated the dismal gloom of

the forest; and then proceeded to collect a sufficient quantity of fuel to last through the night. The fire was kindled just at the mouth of his little shelter, into which he crept with a determination to watch carefully, and keep up his fire, well knowing that if he suffered it to go out, he would probably never wake again. But the fatigue he had gone through during the day, the intense cold he had endured, and the weakness occasioned by long fasting, all combined to produce an irresistible drowsiness, and long before morning he fell asleep. How long he slept he knew not, but when he revived to some degree of consciousness, he was without the use of his limbs; the fire was almost extinguished, and he was unable to raise himself up, or move hand or foot. A horrible apprehension came over him, and the sudden impulse it communicated to the pulsation of the heart, probably saved his life. By degrees he was able to crawl to the fire, which he raked together, and replenished with fuel; and then, by violent exercise, restored the circulation of his blood. In a little while the day broke, the clouds cleared away, and the sun rose bright and clear. By the aid of this sure guide, he was enabled to shape his course towards the river, which having once gained, he could easily find his way back to the village.

It being usual for the Long Finne to stay out all day on his hunting excursions, his absence excited no anxiety until it became dark. The

intense cold had gathered the good Heer and his
family close around a blazing hickory fire, where,
at first, they began 'to wonder what had become
of the youth. By degrees, as the evening advanced,
and the storm grew louder and louder, their apprehensions became painful, and each furnished a
variety of suggestions, to account for his non-
appearance, none of which, however, were satis-
factory. As bed time drew near and he came not,
the fair and gentle Christina could, no longer conceal those keen anxieties which virtuous timidity
had hitherto enabled her to smother in the recesses
of her heart. " He will perish in the snow," cried
she 'in 'agony ; and she besought her father to
alarm the village. Accordingly, a party was collected, some carrying lights, and others guns, to
go into the woods in search of the lost Koningsmarke. They hallooed and fired their guns to no
purpose : no answer was received, except 'from
others of the party ; and about midnight they had
all returned, with a full conviction that the youth
had already perished in the snow. The good Heer
shed tears at the thought of his melancholy fate ;
but the eyes of his fair daughter were dry, while
her heart wept drops of blood.

She retired to her chamber, and gave vent to
her feelings in exclamations of despairing anguish.
" He has perished alone ; he is buried under the
cold snows, and the wolves will devour his dead
corse !" " Better," answered the voice of the

Frizzled Head—"better that he should perish alone, than that others should die for him! better that the wolves should devour him, than that he should devour the innocent lamb! Heaven is just."

"But to perish thus!" exclaimed Christina, wringing her hands.

"It may serve to expiate his crime," answered the Snow Ball. "Better to perish unseen in the depths of the forest, than dangle in the air, a spectacle for the multitude to scorn, and the vultures to peck at l"

"It may be so—it may be so," replied the maiden, "but oh! righteous Providence, would that I had been spared this dreadful, dreadful struggle!"

"Remember," answered the Snow Ball, "remember what he who saved 'thy life caused to her who gave thee thy, life: her spirit watches thee." So saying, she glided out of the room, and poor Christina threw herself on the bed, where she lay till morning, a prey to the most bitter and conflicting emotions.

As the Long Finne was bending his weary course towards the rising sun, he heard the barking of a dog at a distance, which he answered by hallooing aloud. Presently the barking came nearer, and in a few minutes he saw his faithful fox-hound speeding towards him. The poor animal crawled at his feet, wagged his tail, and whined his joy at seeing his master. He then licked his hand, looked up wistfully in his face, and proceeded onwards, every moment turning back, as if to see whether he was followed. Koningsmarke understood all this, and trudged wearily on after, until the sagacious animal led him directly in a straight line to the village.

A hundred shouts from the good people of Elsingburgh hailed his return. The Heer Piper fell on his neck and blessed him ; while his pale daughter, after rushing half way into the room, as if to welcome him, suddenly recoiled, and fainted away. For the first time, did the Heer begin to suspect the state of his daughter's heart; for, although the mysterious hints of the Snow Ball, together with certain occasional sly innuendoes of his long-headed counsellor, Wolfgang Langfanger, had sometimes set him thinking on the subject, he was always called off to the more weighty affairs of state, before he could come to any conclusion on the subject. But the truth flashed upon his mind at once, and his conviction was followed by the exclamation of " *der teufel.*"

Now the Heer was a warm-hearted little man, that came to his conclusions somewhat suddenly. He liked the Long Finne, was accustomed to his society, and, in looking around the village, could see no one worthy the hand of his daughter, or of being son-in-law to the representative of majesty. After reflecting a moment on these matters, he slapped his hand smartly on his thigh, and pronounced, with an air of decision, " It shall be so."

" Long Finne," quoth the Heer—" Long Finne, dost thou love my daughter ?"

" She knows I do," replied the youth, "more than my life."

" Christina, my daughter, my darling, come hither," said the Heer. Christina approached her father, pale as a lily, and trembling like the aspen leaf.

" Christina, art thou willing to be the wife of this youth ? Remember he saved thee from death, and worse perhaps than death. And moreover, he has convinced me that he is nephew to my old friend, Caspar Steinmets."

" And caused the death of—" muttered Bombie to herself, indistinctly, and without being noticed

The poor girl struggled almost to dissolution ; the paleness of death came over her ; she trembled, and sunk on a chair, her head resting on her heaving bosom. The Heer approached, took her cold hand, and said, " Answer me, my daughter ; wilt thou be the wife of this youth ?"

" I will," replied she, gasping for breath.

" Then join your hands," said the good Heer, the tears starting from his eyes, " and receive the blessing of a father."

" And the curses of a mother !" exclaimed Bombie of the Frizzled Head, as she hobbled away.

Christina snatched her hand from the eager grasp of Koningsmarke, and rushed out of the Heer's presence, exclaiming in agony, " Oh, God ! direct me."

" *Der teufel hole* that infernal black Snow Ball," cried the irritated Heer ; " what means the old hag, Long Finne ?"

" She means—she means—that I am—what I pray God thou mayest never be," answered the youth, and rushed out of the room.

" *Der teufel* is in ye all, I think," muttered the Heer Piper, and proceeded to eat his breakfast, out of humour with every body, and particularly with himself. It will generally be found, that a person in this state of mind, at length concentrates his ill humour upon some particular object ; and accordingly it happened that the Heer, by tracing up effects to their causes, discovered that all the mischiefs of the morning originated in Cupid's having, as we before stated, enticed away the Long Finne's dog. Whereupon, he ordered him a sound flogging, at the hands of Lob Dotterel. As the stripes of Boadicea whilome produced a rising of the ancient Britons, so did those of Cupid bring forth results which were long afterward felt by the good people of Elsingburgh.

BOOK FOURTH.

CHAPTER I.

Teaching the true art of genteel writing.

As HISTORY receives a great portion of its dignity and importance, not from the magnitude of those events which it records, but from the rank and consequence of the personages that figure in the great drama of the world, so in like manner doth every work of fiction depend upon the same cause for its interest. Every word and action of a legitimate monarch, for instance, is matter of infinite moment, not only to the present age, but to posterity; and it is consequently carefully recorded in books of history. If he takes a ride, or goes to church, it is considered, especially the latter event, such a rarity that nothing will do but it must be set down in the chronicles.

Hence the vast advantages accruing to an author from a discreet choice of his characters, whose actions, provided they are persons of a proper rank, may be both vulgar and insignificant, without either tiring or disgusting the reader. The hero, provided he is right royal, or even noble, may turn his palace into a brothel, or commit the most paltry meannesses, without losing his character ; and the heroine, if of sufficient rank, may, by virtue of her prerogative, swear like a fishwoman, without being thought in the least vulgar. The most delicate and virtuous female, properly imbued with a taste for the extempore historical novel, does not mind being introduced, by a' popular author, into the company of strumpets, pimps, and their dignified employers, whose titles and patents of nobility give them the privilege of doing things that would dis-grace the vulgar, who, poor souls, have no way of becoming tolerably respectable, but by conforming to the common decencies of life. So also, a Buckingham, a Rochester, or a Sir Charles Sedley, or any other distinguished person, historically witty, may be made by an author as coarse, flat, and vulgar in his conversations, as the said author himself, who puts the words into his mouth, and, ten to one, the reader will think he is banqueting on the quintessence of refined wit and humour. Not to multiply particular instances, we may lay it down as a general rule, that the dignity of actions, the refinement of morals, and the sharpness of wit, is exactly in proportion to the rank and quality of the characters to whom they appertain.

For the reasons above stated, we here take special occasion to remind the reader, that most of our principal characters are fully entitled, by their rank and dignity, to the privilege of being dull and vulgar, without forfeiting his respect or admiration.

The Heer Piper, though not actually a king himself, is the representative of a king. He also held,
or at least claimed, sovereign sway over a space
of country as large at least as Great Britain, and
was as little subject to any laws, except of his own
making, as the most mortal tyrant in Christendom.
We see, therefore, no particular reason why he
may not be allowed to swear, without being thought
indecent, as well as Elizabeth, Harry the Fourth,
or any other swearing potentate on record.

We also claim the benefit of sublimity for the
effusions of Bombie of the Frizzled Head ; who,
as before stated, was the wife and daughter of an
African monarch, superior in state and dignity to
any European legitimate ; because he could actually sell his subjects, whereas the latter are only
entitled to pick their pockets. If it be objected
that she is a slave, we would observe, that this
misfortune, this reverse of fate, only renders her
the more interesting, as exhibiting in her person
an awful example of the uncertainty of all human
grandeur. Kings and queens have often been
bought and sold ; and, as a king of Cyprus was
once publicly exhibited for sale in the market of
Rome, so may it possibly happen, before some of
our readers die, that others, of the race which has
so long domineered over mankind, may be made
to exhibit examples equally striking, of the mutability of fortune. We caution our readers also
to bear in mind, that that likely fellow Cupid has

also a portion of the blood royal in his veins, the effects of which, we trust, will be strikingly exemplified in the course of this history.

If, after all, the reader should object that this is mere secondhand royalty, and be inclined to pronounce the awful condemnation of vulgarity upon us and our book, we here take this opportunity to pledge ourselves, in the course of a few succeeding chapters, to introduce some genuine legitimate monarchs, full-blooded, and with pedigrees equal to that of an Arabian horse, or the renowned Eclipse himself, meaning not, however, to detract either from the merits of Mr. Van Ranst or his horse, by this latter assertion.

CHAPTER II.

Sudden a rush of kings came down like rain,
Made a long speech and then went back again.

Now the laughing, jolly spring, began sometimes to show her buxom face in the bright morning; but ever and anon, meeting the angry frown of winter, loath to resign his rough sway over the wide realm of nature, she would retire again into her southern bower. Yet, though her visits were at first but short, her very look seemed to exercise a magic influence. The buds began slowly to expand their close winter folds; the dark and melancholy woods to assume an almost imperceptible purple tint; and here and there a little chirping bluebird hopped about the orchards of Elsingburgh. Strips of fresh green appeared along the brooks, now released from their icy fetters; and nests of little variegated flowers, nameless, yet richly deserving a name, sprung up in the sheltered recesses of the leafless woods. By and by, the shad, the harbinger at once of spring and plenty, came up the river before the mild southern breeze; the ruddy blossoms of the peach-tree exhibited their gorgeous pageantry; the little lambs appeared frisking and gambolling about the sedate mother; young, innocent calves, began their first bleatings;

the cackling hen announced her daily feat, in the barn-yard, with clamorous exultation ; every day added to the appearance of that active vegetable and animal life, which nature presents in the progress of the genial spring ; and finally, the flowers, the zephyrs, the warblers, and the maidens rosy cheeks, announced to thè eye, the ear, the senses, the fancy, and the heart, the return and the stay of the vernal year.

But the sprightly song, the harmony of nature, the rural blessings, and the awakened charms of spring, failed to bring back peace or joy to the bosom of our blue-eyed maid. Every heart seemed glad save her's ; and the roses grew every where but on the cheek of Christina

Yet, however interested we may be for the repose and happiness of that gentle girl, we are compelled to lose sight of her for awhile, in order to attend to matters indispensable to the progress of our history.

At the period of which we are writing, the whole of both banks of the Delaware, from the Hoarkill, now Lewiston, to Elsingburgh, was in a state of nature. The country had been granted by different monarchs to different persons, who had, from time to time, purchased of the Indians large tracts of country, of which but a very inconsiderable portion, just about their forts, was cultivated. Above Elsingburgh was the settlement of Coaquanock, on the same side of the Delaware ; and higher up was Chygoos, and the Falls settlement, where Trenton now stands. Beyond this, establishments had been formed, and small villages built, at Elizabethtown, Bergen, Middletown, Shrewsbury, Amboy, and perhaps a few other places. With little exceptions, all the settlers dwelt in villages for their security against the Indians, having their farms scattered around, which they cultivated with arms in their hands.

In the intermediate spaces, between these distant settlements, resided various small tribes of Indians, who sometimes maintained friendly relations with their new neighbours, at others committed depredations and murders. The early settlers of this country were, perhaps, as extraordinary a race of people as ever existed. Totally unwarlike in their habits, they ventured upon a new world, and came, few in numbers, fearlessly into the society and within the power of a numerous race of savages. The virtuous and illustrious William Penn, and his followers, whose principles and practice were those of non-resistance, and who held even self-defence unlawful, trusted themselves to the wilds, not with arms in their hands, to fight their way among the wild Indians, but with the olive branch, to interchange the peaceful relations of social life. There was in these adventurers, generally, a degree of moral courage, faith, perseverance, hardihood, and love of independence, civil and religious, that enabled them to do with the most limited means, what,

with the most ample, others have failed in achiev-
ing. We cannot read their early history, and
dwell upon the patient endurance of labours and
dangers on the part of the men, of heroic faith and
constancy on that of the women, without feeling
our eyes moisten, our hearts expand with affectionate admiration of these our noble ancestors, who
watered the young tree of liberty with their tears,
and secured, at the price of their blood, to themselves and their posterity, the noblest of all privi-
leges, that of worshipping God according to their
consciences.

The character of the Indian nations, which inhabited these portions of the country, and indeed
that of all the various tribes of savages in North
America, was pretty uniform. Like all ignorant
people, they were very superstitious. When the
great comet appeared in 1680, a sachem was asked
what he thought of its appearance. " It signifies,"
said he, " that we Indians shall melt away, and this
country be inhabited by another people." They
had a great veneration for their ancient burying-
grounds; and when any of their friends or relatives
died at a great distance, would bring their bones
to be interred in the cemetery of the tribe. Nothing,
in after times, excited a deeper vengeance against
the white people, than their ploughing up the ground
where the bones of their fathers had been deposited.
When well treated, they were kind and liberal to
the strangers; but were naturally reserved, apt to

resent, to conceal their resentment, and retain it a long time. But their remembrance of benefits was equally tenacious, and they never forgot the obligations of hospitality.

In these early days, an old Indian used to visit the house of a worthy farmer at Middletown, in New-Jersey, where he was always hospitably received and kindly entertained. One day the wife of the farmer observed the Indian to be more pensive than usual, and to sigh heavily at intervals. She inquired what was the matter, when he replied, that he had something to tell her, which, if it were known, would cost him his life. On being further pressed, he disclosed a plot of the Indians, who were that night to surprise the village, and murder all the inhabitants. " I never yet deceived thee," cried the old man; " tell thy husband, that he may tell his white brothers; but let no one else know that I have seen thee to-day." The husband collected the men of the village to watch that night. About twelve o'clock they heard the war-whoop; but the Indians, perceiving them on their guard, consented to a treaty of peace, which they never afterward violated.

Their ideas of justice were nearly confined to the revenging of injuries; but an offender who was taken in attempting to escape the punishment of a crime, submitted to the will of his tribe, without a murmur. On one occasion, a chief named Tashyowican lost a sister by the small-pox, the

introduction of which by the whites was one great
occasion of the hostility of the Indians. " The
Maneto of the white man has killed my sister,"
said he, " and I will go kill the white man." Accordingly, taking a friend with him, they set upon
and killed a settler of the name of Huggins. On
receiving information of this outrage, the settlers
demanded satisfaction of the tribe to which Tashyowican belonged, threatening severe retaliation
if it were refused. The sachems despatched two
Indians to take him, dead or alive. On coming to
his wigwam, Tashyowican, suspecting their designs, asked if they intended to kill him. They
replied, " no—but the sachems have ordered you
to die " " And what do you say, brothers ?" replied he. " We say you must die," answered they.
Tashyowican then covered his eyes, and cried out
" kill me," upon which they shot him through the
heart.

Previous to their intercourse with the whites,
they had few vices, as their state of society furnished them with few temptations ; and these vices
were counterbalanced by many good, not to say
great qualities. But, by degrees, they afterward
became corrupted by that universal curse of their
race, spirituous liquors, the seductions of which the
best and greatest of them could not resist. It is
this which has caused their tribes to wither away,
leaving nothing behind but a name, which will soon
be forgotten, or, at best, but a miserable remnant

of degenerate beings, whose minds are debased, and whose forms exhibit nothing of that tall and stately majesty which once characterized the monarchs of the forest.

But the most universal and remarkable trait in the character of the red men of North America, was a gravity of deportment, almost approaching to melancholy. It seemed as if they had a presentiment of the fate which awaited them in the increasing numbers of the white strangers ; and it is certain, that there were many traditions and prophecies among them, which seemed to indicate the final ruin and extinction of their race. Their faces bore the expression of habitual melancholy ; and it was observed that they never laughed or were gay, except in their drunken feasts, which, however, generally ended in outrage and bloodshed. The little Christina always called them THE SAD PEOPLE ; and the phrase aptly expressed their peculiar character.

It is little to be wondered at, if two races of men, so totally distinct in habits, manners, and interests, and withal objects of mutual jealousy, suspicion and fear, should be oftener enemies than friends. Every little singularity observed in the actions and deportment of each other, accordingly gave rise to suspicion, often followed by outrage ; and every little robbery committed on the property of either, was ascribed to the other party, so that the history of their early intercourse with each

other, is little other than a narrative of bickerings
and bloodshed. Thus they continued, until it finally
happened in the new, as it hath always happened
in the old world, that the "wise white man" gained
a final ascendency, and transmitted it to his posterity.

About the period to which our history has now
brought us, there existed considerable misunder-
standing between the Heer Piper and the neighbouring tribes. A mill had been built near the
mouth of the little river, which being dammed
across, the shad and herrings, which formed the
principal portion of their food at this season, could
no longer ascend the stream into the interior of the
country, where the Indians came in the spring to
fish. The Indians had likewise drank up the liquor,
expended the powder, and worn out the watch-
coats they had received for a large territory they
had sold to the Swedish government; and, as usual
on such occasions, began to be sick of their bargain. The sachems also complained that Dominie
Kanttwell had been tampering with some of their
people, and, in attempting to teach them to be good
Christians, had only taught them to drink rum, and
made them bad Indians.

On the other hand, the Heer Piper charged them
with trespassing on the rights of his Swedish majesty, by hunting on the lands ceded by them in
fair purchase. He also hinted his suspicions of a
design on their part to surprise the town of Elsing-

burgh, which suspicion he founded upon some
mysterious hints of the Snow Ball, who of late
had given vent to certain inexplicable obscurities.
Dominie 'Kanttwell, too, was horribly out of humour, in consequence of having been sorely puzzled in ,argument, not long since, by a sly old
sachem whom he attempted to convert to what he
assured him was the only true faith.   The old
sachem listened till he had done, it being their custom never to interrupt any person in speaking, and
then replied with great gravity :—

"Brother, you say your religion is the only true
religion in the world. Good. I have been in Canada,
and there they told me their's was the only true
religion.   Good.   I have been at Boston, where
they assured me the religion of the people of Canada was the religion of the bad spirit, and that
their's was the only true one. Good. I have been
at the Manhattans, where they called the white
people of Boston bad people, and said they had
no religion.   Good.   I have been at Coaquanock,
among the *Big Hats*, and they told me the religion'
of the Manhattans was not the right sort.   Good.
I am here, and you say, brother, our's is the only
good religion, and you must believe like me. Good.
But brother, which am I to believe ? You say, all
of you, that the good book out of which you preach
is what you all take for your guide, and that it is
written by the Great Spirit himself, yet you all
differ among yourselves. Now, brother, hear what

I have got to say. As soon as you shall agree among yourselves which is the true religion, I shall think of joining you. Good."

To explain these apparent contradictions to the capacity of a man of nature, was out of the question. Indians cannot comprehend metaphysical subtilties, and the religion calculated for a state of society like their's, must be composed of the most simple elements. However this may be, the Dominie resented the obstinacy of the old sachem, and actually talked of converting the savages with fire and sword. The Heer, however, preferred calling a conference with some of the chiefs, who were accordingly summoned to meet the representative of the Swedish majesty, at a spot about four miles from Elsingburgh, on the bank of the little river to which we have so often alluded in the course of this history.

The place selected for this meeting was a little flat in a curve of the river, which was here about twenty yards wide, clothed with majestic elms and sycamores, standing at various distances from each other, and without any underwood. The greensward extended to the edge of the stream on one side, and on the other rose a lofty barrier of rocks, clothed with gray mosses, and laurel bushes now just exhibiting their pale pink blossoms. The precipice was crowned, at its summit, with a primeval growth of lofty oaks that waved their broad arms beyond the rocks, and partly overshadowed the stream, which, a little onward, wound between two high hills and disappeared.

To this sequestered spot came the Heer Piper, accompanied by the Long Finne, Dominie Kanttwell, the trusty counsellors of Elsingburgh, together with divers men, women, and children, drawn thither by curiosity, and whom the indefatigable Lob Dotterel kept in order, by dint of making more noise than all the rest. Here, too, came ten or a dozen of the monarchs of the new world, whose names and titles, translated into English, equal those of the most lofty and heaven-born kings of the east. There came the Big Buffalo, the Little Duck Legs, the Sharp Faced Bear, the Walking Shadow, the Rolling Thunder, the Iron Cloud, the Jumping Sturgeon, the Belly Ache, and the Doctor, all legitimate sovereigns, with copper rings in their noses, blanket robes of state, and painted faces. These were accompanied by a train of inferior chiefs and warriors, who seated themselves in silence, in a half circle, on one side of the little plain. On the right of these sat the kings, their bodies bent forward in a posture to listen, and their blankets drawn closely around their shoulders, which, when occasionally opened, disclosed the deadly tomahawk and scalping knife.

On the opposite side, upon a little natural platform, was placed a bench, or tribune, for the Heer Piper and his suite. The Heer on this occasion was dressed in his uniform as a Swedish officer, which he wore under the great Gustavus, and had on a sword, given him, as he affirmed, by that bulwark of the Protestant faith, as a reward for certain great services, which Governor Piper declined to enumerate, except on new-year's eve, and other remarkable epochs. The Rolling Thunder produced a long pipe, ornamented with dyed horse hair, porcupine's quills variously coloured, and many enormous devices. Having lighted it, he took a whiff or two, handed it to the next, and thus it passed completely round the circle, till both white men and red men had partaken in the solemn rite of peace. The Rolling Thunder then bowed gracefully to the Heer, and waved his hand in token that they were ready to hear him. Governor Piper rose, and his speech was from time to time translated by an interpreter.

"Delawares, Minks, Mingoes, Muskrats, and Mud Turtles, listen!" said the Heer, feeling all the dignity of his situation as the representative of a king, addressing an assemblage of kings.

"You have behaved badly of late; you have sold lands, and taken them back again, after you had shot away your powder, emptied your tobacco-boxes, and drank your rum.

"Delawares, Minks, Mingoes, Muskrats, and Mud Turtles, listen!

"You grow worse every day, notwithstanding the trouble we take to make you better; you get drunk and fight each other with knives, instead of embracing like brothers. This is wicked, and the Great Spirit will punish you. Before many moons are passed away, people will ask what has become of the Delawares, the Mingoes, and the rest of the red men? and the answer shall be, they have been consumed in liquid fires.

"Delawares, Minks, Mingoes, Muskrats, and Mud Turtles, listen!

"You have refused to hear those whom I sent amongst you, to teach you the worship of the true Great Spirit, who is angry with you, and has sent the small-pox to punish your obstinacy. You have hunted on the white man's ground, and broke down the dam I caused to be built across the river, that we might grind our corn, and saw boards to build our houses. These are some of the things I wished to talk to you about. The Great Spirit, I tell you, is angry, and your great father, across the big lake yonder, will take vengeance. Let me hear what you have to say."

The red kings heard this harangue in dead silence, and waited a little while to see if the Heer had done speaking. The Rolling Thunder then rose, and, throwing back his blanket, so as to bare his shoulder and red right arm, spoke as follows, beginning in a low tone, and gradually becoming more loud and animated:—

"Long Knife! The strong liquor was first brought among us by the Dutch, who sold it to us, and then told us we must not drink it; they knew it was for our hurt, yet they tempted us to buy it.

"Long Knife! The next people that came among us was the English, who likewise sold us strong liquors, which they blamed us afterward for drinking. The next that came were the Swedes, your people, and they too sold us strong drinks. All of you knew they were hurtful to us, and that if you let us have them, we would drink them, and become mad. We drink, abuse one another, and throw each other into the fire. Six score and ten of our people have been killed by their own brothers, in these mad fits of drinking. Who is to blame for this?

"Long Knife! You say, that after we have made away with the price of our lands, we come there and hunt on them as if they were our own. We sold you the land, and the trees upon it, but we did not sell the fowls of the air, and the beasts of the forest. These belong to those who have courage and skill to catch them. The Long Knives don't know how to hunt any more than women.' You say, too, that we have destroyed the dam which you made across the river to grind your corn. This spring, when we were looking out for the fish to come up the river as they used to do, none came, and our women and children were near starving. We came down to see what was the matter, and found the fish could not get up your dam, so we destroyed it. You tell us that men should do as they would be done by. Why then did you deprive us of fish, that you might grind your corn?

" Long Knife! We have listened to the Dominie's talks, and tried to understand them, but we cannot. The Great Spirit has given the red men one mind, and the white men another. When you bargain with us for three beaver skins, you will not take one for three; yet you want us to believe that three Great Spirits make but one Great Spirit. We can't understand this. Is that our fault?

" Long Knife! You say we grow worse and worse every day, and that the Great Spirit will, in his anger, sweep us from the face of the earth. We know this, for already our numbers are growing less and less every day. The white man is the fire which is lighted in the woods, and burns up the leaves, and kills the tall trees of the forest. We shall perish, or be driven before it, till we come to where the sun sets in the great salt lake of the west, and when we can go no farther, there will soon be an end of our race. If such is the will of the Great Spirit, we cannot help it; if it is not his will, you cannot make it so.

" Long Knife! I have answered you; now, hear me. You came here as strangers, but few in number, and asked us for a little piece of land for a garden—we gave it you. By-and-by, you asked for more, and it was given. When we were tired of giving, you purchased of us great tracts of country for tobacco-boxes and rum. The tobacco-boxes and rum are gone, and you have the land. Is it any wonder that we are angry at being made fools of, 'and wish to have our lands back again? Every day the white man comes, and pushes the Indian farther and farther back into the woods, where there are neither fish nor oysters to eat. Is it any wonder that, when we are hungry, we fall into bad humours and hate the white men? The Dominie tells us that you have a right to our country, because we don't make fences, plough up the ground, and grow rich and happy, like your people, in their own country. ' If they were so happy at home, I don't see why they came here.

"Long Knife! We would like to be friends with you, but you are a bad people; you have two faces, two hearts, and two tongues; you tell us one thing, and you do another: a red man never lies, except when you have made him drunk; what he says, he will do; he never crosses his track. You came here as friends, but you have been our worst enemies; you brought us strong drink, small-pox, and lies: 'go home again, and take these all back with you. We would, if possible, be as we once were, before you came amongst us. Go! leave us to our woods, our waters, our ancient customs, and our ancient gods. If the Great Spirit wishes us to plough the land, sell rum, and become Christians, he can do it. But the means you take will only bring these things about, when there will be nothing left of the red men but their name, and their graves."

When the Rolling Thunder ceased, Dominie Kanttwell arose and made a speech, which, however zealous and well meant, only served to exasperate the red kings. He treated their ancient belief with scorn; insulted their feelings of national pride; scoffed at their modes of thinking and acting; and drew a mortifying contrast betwixt the ignorant barbarian roaming the woods, and the white man enjoying the comfort and security of civilized life. The surrounding Indians began to murmur; then to gnash their teeth, and finally many of them, starting up, seized their tomahawks, and uttered the war-whoop. The Heer and his party were now in imminent danger of falling victims to the fury of the moment. But the *Rolling Thunder* arose, and, waving his hand for silence, spoke as follows :—

"Red men!—hear me! The Long Knives came here in peace, so let them depart. Let us not imitate their treachery, by taking advantage of their confidence to destroy them. Behold! I here extinguish the pipe of peace; I break the belt of wampum, that was the symbol of our being friends, and dig up the buried tomahawk. We are friends no more. Long Knife, go hence in peace to-day, but to-morrow count the red men thy mortal foes. Before another moon is past, look to see me again."
He then bared his arm, and, drawing his knife,

stuck it into the fleshy part. The blood spouted forth as he exclaimed, " For every drop that now falls to the ground there- shall be counted one, two, three, ay, four victims, from the nest of the serpent."

The red kings then slowly moved off, followed by their people, who gradually disappeared, yelling the war-whoop, and chanting bloody songs, till at length their voices died away in the recesses of the forest. The alarmed and irritated Heer muttered to himself *"Verflucht und verdamt sey deine schwarze seele,"* and, together with his tram, returned gloomy and dissatisfied to his village of Elsingburgh.

CHAPTER III.

" The spit that stood behind the door,
　Threw the pudding-stick down on the floor;
　Odsplut! says the gridiron, can't you agree?
　I'm THE HEAD CONSTABLE, bring 'em to me."
　　　　　　　　　　Mother Goose's Melodies.

LIKE the old war-horse, when he snuffs the scent
of powder, hears the shrill fife, the braying trumpet,
and the thrilling drum, the Heer Piper now felt the
spirit of the ancient follower of the great Gustavus
reviving within him, even as the snuff of an expiring
lamp or candle; the latter being rather the most
savoury comparison.　He inspected his palisades,
scoured his pattereroes, victualled his garrison, and
exercised the villagers in practising the deadly
rifle.　Every day he invested himself in his cocked-
hat, invincible sword, and tarnished regimentals,
and strutted about with a countenance so full of
undaunted valour, that the very women and little
children slept soundly every night, save when a
troop of howling wolves approached the village
under cover of darkness, and waked them with
the apprehension of an attack of the Indians, led
on by the Rolling Thunder himself, whose very
name was enough to alarm a whole regiment of
militia.

One of the most provoking things which mortal

man encounters in this spiteful world, is taking **a**
vast deal of trouble to provide against a danger
which never arrives. Yet nothing is more common
than to see people laying up treasures they never
live to enjoy; providing against exigencies that
never happen; and sacrificing present ease, pleasure, and enjoyment, only to guard against the
wants of a period that they never live to see.

It would almost seem that fate delights to mortify the pride of human wisdom, by exhibiting daily
examples, how often the most watchful prudence is
either idly employed in guarding against evils that
never come, or in vainly attempting to evade the
consequences of those that do; while, on the other
hand, the most daring disregard to calculations of
the future is often coupled with the most prosperous
success. We would give that world of fancy,
which is the only world to which we heroes of the
quill can lay any positive claim, to be able to decide the question betwixt the relative prospects
of a person of extraordinary prudence, and no
prudence at all. Possibly, however, the course of
our history may throw some light upon this matter.

More than a fortnight elapsed, amid the din of
preparation, and the vigilance of watchful alarm,
without any appearance of the Rolling Thunder
and his painted warriors. Every day the Heer
talked and strutted more loftily than the day before,
and boasted more confidently of the sound drubbing
he would give these *galgen schivenkels,* if they

dared to attack his fortress of Elsingburgh. But, alas! that man should always be passing from one extreme to another, from the fearfulness of apprehension, to the fool-hardihood of unbounded carelessness. Finding the Indians did not come as soon as he expected them, the good Heer at length persuaded himself they would not come at all, though he ought to have known that the race of the red men come like death, when least expected. He accordingly remitted his vigilance by degrees, and put his fortress upon the peace establishment, in spite of the singular and mysterious warnings of the Frizzled Head. That declamatory oddity was now more vehement than ever in her incomprehensible denunciations, never meeting the Heer without uttering some dismal raven's note.

" Sleep on, till thou wakest no more," cried she ; " dream till thy dreamings end in waking woes; and believe that what is not, will never be."

" What meanest thou, thou eternal mill-clapper ?" would the Heer reply ; " away with thee, and either speak what thou knowest, or hold thy tongue, What knowest thou ? *der teufel hole dich.*"

" I know what I know—I could tell what I will not tell—I could save those I love, at the risk of losing those that I love still better."

" Confound thee for a muddle-pated, crack-brained Snow Ball," quoth the Heer ; while Bombie of the Frizzled Head would go in search of that likely fellow Cupid, her grandson, who every day became more moody and ungovernable, and now spent more than half his time wandering about with his dog in the woods. These two were observed to have frequent conferences together, in which Bombie sometimes seemed greatly agitated; but the subject of their discussions was not known, as they excited little interest.

Whitsuntide came, and with it a hundred rural sports, and sprightly merry-makings. The buxom lasses, with gayest gear, and cheeks redder than the rose, accompanied by many a rustical and barbarous Corydon, hied forth to the woods, in search of *Pinckster apples*, or to play at hide-and-seek among the blossoms. The boys, and lads who were yet too young to think of sweethearts, were gathered together in a large level common, just without the village, pursuing such various sports as inclination led them to prefer. In one place, a party of lusty lads were playing at ball, having for audience some half a dozen black fellows, who applauded with obstreperous admiration any capital stroke or feat in running. Elsewhere, a party not quite old enough to be admitted among the others, 'were amusing themselves in pairs, by striking their balls from one to the other. A third set were shooting marbles; a fourth firing little lead cannons; a fifth setting off *ascotches*, as they are 'yclept in boyish parlance; a sixth was playing at chuck-farthing, with old buttons without eyes; a seventh rolling in the dirt; and an eighth, making dirt pies. In short, there was no end to the diversity of sports ; it was holyday, and all were happy as noise and freedom could make them.

The only drawback upon the pleasures of these merry and noisy wights, was the presence of that busybody Lob Dotterel, the high constable of Elsingburgh, who never saw a knot of people, great or small, making merry together, that he was not in the thickest of them, causing mischief, and spoiling sport, by what he was pleased to denominate keeping the peace. We should have mentioned before, that among the plans adopted by the Heer and his trusty counsellors for improving the police of Elsingburgh, was that of passing ordinances for the prevention of various amusements, which children have practised from time immemorial, and which are as much their right, as any of the immunities which men enjoy under the common law. If Lob Dotterel, who was always on the look-out, brought information that a horse had thrown his rider in consequence of being frightened by a paper kite, a law was forthwith enacted to forbid that dangerous and unlawful practice ; if an old woman chanced to have her petticoat singed by the explosion of an ascotch, an ordinance was straightway fulminated against these pestilent fireworks ; and so on till the urchins of the village were gradually so hemmed in by laws, that, if they had paid any attention to these enactments, the little rogues would hardly have had an amusement, or a play

that was not unlawful. Like many modern legis-
lators of the present time, a single fact was sufficient ground for passing half a dozen great wordy
laws, which, after all, nobody obeyed. These, for
the most part, lay dormant, like a great spider in
the recesses of his web, until the zeal of some Lob
Dotterel would sally out upon some little buzzing
fly of a boy, who had chanced to get entangled in
their mazes.

It was amazing to see the bustling activity of
Lob, on this occasion of the sports of Whitsuntide.
If two little fellows happened to fall out in playing
at marbles, or chuck-farthing, and proceeded to
settle the dispute, by an appeal to the law of nature ; or if a hubbub was raised in any part of the
field, that indefatigable officer dashed in among
them ; and wherever he came, there was an awful
silence, till he was called to some other quarter,
to quell another riot, when his departure was announced by a renewal of the fight and noise. Never
was poor man in such a worry ; and never did
poor man get so little for his pains, as Lob Dotterel,
who might be said to be in the predicament of
certain great conquerors, or rather, of certam
legitimate monarchs, of the present day, who, the
moment they have quelled an insurrection in one
part of their territories, are straightway called to
another for the like purpose. Various were the
tricks put upon the high constable. At one time,
they pinned a dishclout to the skirt of his coat, with

which he marched about for a time, unknowing
of this appendage to his dignity ; at another, they
exploded an ascotch under his tail ; and at a third,
they pelted him behind his back with a shower of
dirt and missiles of various kinds. It was in vain
that he turned round to punish the delinquent, for
at the instant, the fry dispersed like a flock of birds,
and others attacked his rear with some new annoyance. Never man in authority was so baited and
worried in the exercise of his office as Lob Dotterel, who finally quitted the field, disgusted with
official dignity, leaving the small fry of Elsingburgh
to play at ball, shoot marbles, fly kites, chuck-far-
things, roll in the dirt, and fight rough and tumble,
uninterrupted, all day long.

Towards sunset, the Heer, who had a certain
mellowness about him that caused his heart to
curvet and caper at the sight of human happiness,
came out with honest Ludwig Varlett, who sym-
pathised in such sports as these, to renovate his
age with a sight of the lusty gambols. While thus
employed, he was assailed by the Frizzled Head,
who hovered near him, and poured forth a more
than usual quantity of incomprehensibilities. Sometimes she addressed the Heer, and at others, turning towards the sportive groups, she would apos-
trophize them in seeming abstraction.

" Yes," muttered she, " yes, sport away, ye
grasshoppers, that die dancing and singing ! The
cricket chirps in the hearth when the house is on

fire; the insect sports in the noonday sun, and dreams not of the coming midnight frost that lays him stiff and cold."

Then, turning to the governor, she would exclaim, with earnest energy—

"Heer! Heer!—Thou seest the sun going down yonder in the west; take heed lest you never see it rise again. Remember that danger comes like a thief in the night, and that the perils of sleep are greater than those of waking. To-morrow—who knows which of us shall see to-morrow?—to-morrow we may be, like yesterdav, a portion of eternity. Remember, and despise not thy last warning!"

The sun went down; the chilly dews damped the grass and the hilarity of the sportful groups, that gradually broke away and returned to the village.

All that evening Bombic hovered about her master, as if impelled by some inscrutable impulse, and seeming to wish to say what she dared not utter.

"*Der teufel hole dich*," said the Heer at last; "What wouldst thou? I believe thou hast swallowed too much liquor, and art drunk."

"The spirit moves me," she slowly replied, "but it is not that spirit which is the curse of our race and thine."

"Then let it move thee to talk so as to be understood; say out, or say nothing, thou croaking raven."

"Yes—I am the raven whose notes forebode and forewarn: when the raven croaks, let the mortal at whose windows he flutters, beware; when Bombie croaks, do thou too beware, Heer."

"Of what?"

"Of—I cannot tell. To save the blood of those who have been kind to me, at least sometimes, I should shed blood that runs in the veins of the only being that claims kindred with me in this wide world. Heer, I have warned thee, farewell. When thou hearest the murderous yell, the dying shriek, the shout of triumph, and the crackling flames, blame not me.—Farewell!"

So saying, she slowly retired, and he saw her no more. The Heer pondered for a moment on her strange warnings; but he had been so accustomed to her wild and wayward talk, that the impression soon passed away. He retired to rest, and was soon in his usual profound sleep, the result of good health and a good conscience.

CHAPTER IV.

The wolf and weasel roam at night,
  Aye seeking bloody prey ;
The ghosts come out in sheet of white,
  But man is worse than they.
                    The Robbing of the Roost.

NIGHT, that gives to the honest man rest, and
rouses the rogue, the wolf, and the owl, to their
predatory labours, now held her quiet sway over
the peaceful inhabitants of the village. The vigilant sentinels, whose turn it was to watch at the
gates of the palisades, which surrounded the place,
were fast asleep at their posts, like their legitimate
successors, the trusty watchmen of New-York and
Philadelphia ; and nothing disturbed the repose of
midnight but the barkings of some sleepless curs,
baying each other from afar. Not a soul was
awake in the village save the mysterious Frizzled
Head, who wandered about from the kitchen to
the hall, and back again, muttering and mumbling
her incomprehensible, disjointed talk. Suddenly
she stopped before the great clock, and, contemplating it for a moment, exclaimed, " The hour is
almost come. Now is the time, or never. I may
yet save my master and his child without betray-
ing my own blood."

So saying, she hobbled up to the chamber of the
Long Finne, and, shaking him till he awoke, ex-

claimed, " Arise, Koningsmarke ; the wolves are approaching. Awake, or thy sleep will last for ever."

" What of the wolves?" answered he, rubbing his eyes ; " are they abroad to-night near the village ?"

" Yes, the wolves that carry the tomahawk and scalping knife, that devour not the innocent lambs, but drink the blood of thy race. Ere half an hour is passed away you will hear the Rolling Thunder rattling, not in the clouds, but at thy door. Quick, arm thyself, and awaken the people that sleep on the brink of the grave. Be quick, I say ; the Indians are out to-night."

Koningsmarke dressed himself hastily, seized his sword and rifle, and sallied forth to alarm the village ; while Bombie went and roused the Heer, who bestowed upon her his benediction, for thus disturbing his slumbers. When, however, he was assured by the Frizzled Head, who for once condescended to be explicit, that the savages were abroad, he hastily dressed himself in his cocked-hat and rusty regimentals, girded on his sword, and hastened to perform the duties of his station. But ere half the men of the village were dressed, the great clock in the palace-hall struck twelve, and at that moment a horrible yell that rose from every quarter, announced that the place was surrounded by the savage warriors. That yell, which the adventurous founders of the new world were, alas! too well accustomed to hear, roused all but the dead. All now was confusion, noise, and hor-ror; yet still the hardy spirits of the villagers did not yield to despair. Every man waited at his post, and even the women and children stood ready to load the guns, and hand them to their brave defenders.

The little village of Elsingburgh was built close to the river, so that one part of the entrenchment, which consisted of thick palisades, about fourteen feet high, with loop-holes at equal distances for firing upon assailants, and strongly fastened to two rows of beams in the inner side, with locust-tree nails, was immersed in the water four or five feet at high tides. Here the fishing boats belonging to the villagers were drawn in every night, to secure them against theft, or injury from any quarter. This side of the village being in some degree pro-tected by the river, the Indians bent all their efforts to set fire to the palisades, and force the gate, which looked towards the country.

Led on by the Rolling Thunder, the Indians assailed the gate, where fought the valiant Heer, seconded by Koningsmarke, and others of the stoutest of his people, with all the arts with which their limited modes of warfare furnished them. They essayed to set the gate on fire, by piling dry brush and wood against the outside; but the women and children brought water, which was handed to those who ventured upon the upper

beams we have described, who threw it upon the
flames, and extinguished them from time to time.
Several times did the fire catch to the dry palisades, and as often was it put out, by the unremitting exertions of those inside. The valiant Elsing-
burghers kept up an incessant fire through the
loop-holes; but the obscurity of the night prevented
their taking deadly aim, although now and then a
yell announced that a shot had taken effect.

Baffled in their attempts to fire the palisades, the
savages now brought large stones, and, piling them
up against the outside, attempted from thence to
climb to the top, and thus jump into the area within.
But the marksmen were on the watch, and the
moment of the appearance of a head above the
palisades, was the signal of death to the assailant.
The Indians have little perseverance in war, and
soon become discouraged by resistance. Their
efforts now began to flag; when, all at once, an
explosion from the little magazine where the powder was deposited, announced to the horror struck
villagers, that their great means of defence was
annihilated in one instant. A groan from within,
and a shout from without the defences, announced
the despair of the white men, and the triumph of
the savages.

The gallant Heer, perceiving now that all was
lost, and that the daylight, now just peering in the
east, would witness the massacre of himself, his
daughter, and his people, motioned to Konings-

marke to go and open the gate towards the river, prepare the boats, and embark the women and children, with all possible speed, while he himself attempted still to make good the defence of the western gate. With silent celerity these orders were obeyed, and Koningsmarke returned in a few minutes, to say that all was ready. "Go now," said the Long Finne, "while Ludwig Varlett, Lob Dotterel, and I, make a stand here, until you are safe." "*Der teufel*," quoth the Heer, "go thou —I must be the last man that deserts his post;— away." "Nay," said the other, "you are old, and cannot run like us; remember thy daughter, thy only daughter. If thou shouldst perish, who will protect her?" "Thou," said the Heer; "remember, if any thing happens to me, I leave her as my dying legacy. Farewell; we must lose no more time in disputing who shall go. When you hear a gun, come speedily."

The Heer and the rest now hastily pursued their way towards the boats, leaving Koningsmarke with his two companions, to make a last stand, for the safety of their poor villagers. The gate was now in a blaze, and, being battered with large stones, as well as weakened by the fire, began to creak and totter fearfully, when the signal was fired. At that moment the gate fell inward. The Indians gave a shout, and waited half a minute to let the burning cinders disperse. That half minute enabled Koningsmarke and his companions to gain a decisive advantage. They fled, pursued by some of the foremost savages, one of whom seized the queue of Lob Dotterel, who luckily wore a wig, which he left in the hands of the astonished warrior as a trophy. The three fugitives jumped into the boat, where was the fair Christina and some two or three women and children, and pushed it off after the others, which had drawn off to some distance. A tall Indian rushed into the water after the last boat, and seized hold of the gunwale with his left hand, grasping his tomahawk in his right. Koningsmarke hastened to the bow with his sword, and with a well-aimed blow cut off the hand that detained the boat. The savage then seized her by the other, which was cut off at the same instant by Koningsmarke. The Indian yelled with rage and fury, and, as the last effort of despair, seized by the side of the boat with his teeth, where he maintained his hold, till his head was severed from his body, and he fell dead into the blood-dyed waters.

But his efforts were fatal to the party in the boat, by enabling several other Indians to rush into the river and seize her at various points. " Make no further resistance, and your lives will be spared; fight, and you die," exclaimed the voice of the Frizzled Head from the shore. Christina, in this moment of terror, threw her white arms around Koningsmarke, and conjured him to listen to the warning. Reluctantly he yielded; the boat was drawn ashore, and the party made prisoners by the Indians, among whom appeared that likely fellow Cupid, who was now seen for the first time, during the whole of this eventful night. Bombie kissed the hand of her young mistress, while the tears rolled down her withered cheeks, and, turning to the Long Finne, exclaimed with solemn earnestness, "The lamb is committed to thee as its shepherd; prove not a wolf to devour it, but watch by day and by night; let not thine eye wink, or thine ear close for a moment, but watch, watch, watch, like the stars that never sleep. Be faithful, and the spirit of the sainted mother may yet forgive the preserver of the daughter." Koningsmarke placed his hand on his heart, lifted his eyes to heaven, and then bowing to the earth, replied in a low voice, "So help me God."

Scarce had the boats which held the fugitives of Elsingburgh rowed out of the reach of the savages, when a cloud of smoke rose on the bosom of the night, succeeded by an hundred rising wreaths of fire, that announced the swift destruction of the homes of the poor villagers. They sat in their boats, weeping and wringing their hands, as one by one the roofs fell in, and the blazing cinders flew aloft in showers of glittering atoms.

The good Heer, who was unconscious that a still heavier calamity had fallen on his aged head, viewed with silent sorrow the destruction of the little nestling place, which, in his hours of proud anticipation, he had pictured as the future capital of a vast empire, of which he would be hailed as the founder. When nothing remained of the village but the ruins, a wild, shrill whoop announced the triumph and departure of the savages, who, just before the rising of the sun, set forth, with exulting hearts, for their forest homes.

As the day advanced, the fugitives ventured to approach the place where their dwellings once stood. Slowly and cautiously they neared the shore, and, perceiving no traces of the Indians, ventured to land among the smoking ruins. Nothing remained of their homes but their ashes, and, like the Israelites, they only returned to weep. Each had suffered in common with the others, and while some uttered loud exclamations of grief, others stood stupified with overwhelming despair.

But the unfortunate Heer, on discovering, for the first time, when they came to the shore, that his daughter was missing, was like one distracted. He ran about in an agony of sorrow, blaming every body, accusing every one of negligence, and himself most of all. Striking his wrinkled forehead, he cried out—" My daughter ! Oh, my daughter ! my only, my beloved child, where art thou now ? Alas ! thy bones are now whitening in these smoking ashes ; or thou art a wretched captive among cruel savages, who will not spare a hair of thine innocent head. And Koningsmarke too ! they have perished together, and would to God I had died with them."

ι " They are not dead," cried a voice, which announced the presence of the Frizzled Head; " they are not dead ; they are carried into captivity, and one day thou mayest perhaps see thy daughter again."

" I shall die," replied the Heer, " long before she comes back to me ;" and he tore his gray hairs, and would not be comforted, although aunt Edith assured him it was the Lord's doing, and therefore it was sinful to repine.

" Alas !" said the sorrowing parent, " the same being gave me an only daughter, and a father's heart to love her. It cannot be a sin to weep the loss of what he gave me." Aunt Edith called this blasphemy, and began to lecture him upon the wickedness of permitting poor Christina to dance and sing. But he heard her not—he stood half bent in the stupor of overwhelming grief, the image of withered, woful despair.

But that salutary necessity for exertion which was given to man, not as a punishment, but a solace and an eventual cure for calamity, did not permit the poor houseless villagers to indulge in the idleness of grief. Without food and shelter, and almost out of the reach of those kindly offices of good neighbourhood, which, in more thickly settled countries, soon help to repair the sudden calamities of life, they must depend on their own resources

to supply their wants. Accordingly, like the indefatigable hornets, who, when their nest is demolished by schoolboys, straightway set about rebuilding it again, our villagers began preparing some
temporary shelter. They erected bowers of the
branches of trees, and made their beds of leaves.
Some employed themselves in fishing, others in
hunting, and all were busy even unto the Dominie,
who went about comforting the people with the assurance that the burning of the village and the loss
of their friends was a judgment upon them for the
unseemly sports they had permitted their children
to indulge in at Whitsuntide. But it was observed,
that those who most strenuously supported this
doctrine when the judgments fell upon their neighbours, found it rather unpalatable, now that they
themselves shared in the calamity.

Perceiving this to be the case, Dominie Kanttwell talked about turning misfortunes into blessings;
the privations of the body to the fattening of the
spirit, and the calamities of this world into rejoic-
ings. The saints of old, he told them, fasted whole
days, nay, sometimes weeks, in voluntary penance;
and were accustomed to sleep in the woods or open
fields, only to mortify the sinful lusts of the flesh.
But for all this, the Dominie's house was the first
that was rebuilt; the Dominie had always the fat-
test fish, and the choicest piece of venison; and
before the village was half rebuilt, aunt Edith went

round with a subscription to purchase him a new gown, and a silver watch, that he might know when it was time to go to meetings.

The day but one after the burning of the village, the Heer was surprised by a visit from his old enemy, Shadrach Moneypenny, accompanied by a good number of *Big Hats*, in boats, bringing with them a supply of food, boards, timber, and other necessaries, together with mechanics to assist them in rebuilding their houses. All these were sent by the good William Penn, who, hearing of their calamity, had opened—no, his heart was always open—had sent them this timely relief. Shadrach was not quite so dry and stiff as at his former visit, and when he appeared in the Heer's presence, paid that respect to his misfortunes which he had denied to his prosperity, by coming as near to making a bow as his canons of courtesy would permit.

" Friend Piper," quoth Shadrach, and the term friend, which had formerly sounded so uncouth, was now grateful to the ear of the broken down parent—" Friend Piper, I come from thy neighbour William Penn, who hath heard of thy misfortune, and sent thee the little he can spare for the relief of thy people."

" But I cannot pay for these, and thy people are said to expect payment for every thing."

" Friend Piper," replied Shadrach, " it may be

that when our people make bargains in the way of business, they are earnest for payment; but when they administer to the sufferings, or contribute to relieve the calamities of their fellow creatures, they expect not to be repaid in this world. William Penn freely bestows upon thee what I have brought; and moreover, bids me say he will send to the Indians, by the first opportunity, to seek, and, if possible, recover thy lost child."

The ancient prejudices of the Heer against his peaceable neighbours of Coaquanock now rushed to his heart, and were there buried for ever in a flood of gratitude. The mention of his daughter, combined with the generous gifts and never broken promises of William Penn, overpowered the old father, and he wept aloud. When his emotions had somewhat subsided, he took Shadrach's hand and said, " Friend, I cannot thank thee." " There is no need, friend Piper. All that William Penn asks of thee, is that thou wilt believe that men were not made, like the beasts of the forest, only to shed each other's blood." The Heer stood corrected, for he remembered the sneers he had thrown out against his peaceable neighbours, the *Big Hats* of Coaquanock.

Aided by these good people, whom the spirit moved to second zealousy the exertions of those of Elsingburgh, that village was renewed, and swarmed again like a bee-hive. The Heer and his subjects long retained a grateful recollection of the kindness of the good William Penn, with the exception, however, of the Dominie and aunt Edith, who were accustomed to flout all good works, and to despise the kind offices of all, save those whom they were pleased to denominate the *elect*.

BOOK FIFTH.

CHAPTER I.

Of demonology and witchcraft in writing.

NOTWITHSTANDING the testimony of King James the First, Cotton Mather, and divers other unquestionable authorities, backed by the opinions of a good portion of mankind, in all time passed, there are a vast many philosophers of this unbelieving age, who affect to doubt the existence of witchcraft, or diabolism, in the affairs of this world. There is no use in arguing with such sturdy unbelievers. We will therefore content ourselves with expressing a firm conviction, that this influence does exist even at this present time ; and that its effects are every day to be seen, more especially in certain highly gifted persons being thereby enabled to perform tasks, which in the ordinary limits of the human faculties, would be quite impossible.

In no instance does this diabolical, or magical power, this direct influence of what Sir Walter Scott calls " gramarye," appear so evident to us, as in the ease with which certain great authors produce those immortal works, that succeed each other with the rapidity of the discharges of a repeating gun. Indeed, if we look back to the first invention of printing, an art which may be said to be the parent of authorship, we shall trace it to this diabolical influence, in the case of the renowned Doctor Faustus, whose power of multiplying books was universally ascribed to the direct agency of gramarye, and who to this day is familiarly coupled with the spirit of darkness. Nay, the doctor, according to unquestionable tradition, was finally carried away, in consequence of a compact, the conditions of which every body is acquainted with. This origin of the art is commemorated in the singular fact, that a certain class of persons employed in the printing-offices are to this day familiarly called printer's devils, indubitably with reference to this diabolical origin of the art. The name of this mischievous and evil disposed familiar, or bad spirit, who inspired Doctor Faustus, was Mephostophilos, as we learn from old Christopher Marlow.

That this same Mephostophilos still exercises great influence in the affairs of authors and printers, and occasionally contracts to lend his assistance on certain conditions, is, we think, sufficiently apparent in the case of various great writers now living, who, not to be profane, certainly write as if the d—l were in them. Some we behold committing the most foul offences against our mortal enemy, common sense; others exhibiting unquestionable proofs of the inspiration which animates them, by attacking and tearing to pieces, the characters of men, women, and little children, and thus committing the most wanton depredations on the scanty stock of human happiness. But if the truth must be ventured upon, in no class of writers do we see this diabolical spirit so clearly evinced, as among the critics, who, not to speak irreverently of these dispensers of fame, do certainly display a most horrible propensity to wickedness, in mauling and cutting up innocent authors, with as little remorse as if they were so many cabbages or pumpkins.

The gentle and courteous reader has, doubtless, long before this, discovered that we ourselves deal in no such wicked compacts, and that we lay claim to no inspiration but what is honestly come by at least. No motive of profit or convenience can possibly induce us to make any covenant with Mephostophilos or any other evil disposed enormity, or to introduce our readers to a fellowship with any being more mischievous than an author. So far from this, we will for the present take our leave of him, with an honest, old-fashioned benediction on his house and all within it, which, in truth, may not be altogether superfluous, seeing

there be so many evil spirits abroad now-a-days,
both in prose and poetry.

> " Saint Francis and Saint Benedight,
> Blesse this house from wicked wight,
> From the nightmare and the goblin,
> That is hight Good Fellow Robin ;
> Keep it from all evil spirits,
> Fairies, weasels, rats, and ferrets,
> From curfew time
> To the next prime."

CHAPTER II.

" Through untrack'd woods, a weary way,
  They wander'd with great pain ;
  And some that went forth on that day,
  Never return'd again."

AFTER the savages had completed the plunder-
ing and burning of the village, they departed with
their prisoners towards the river, on whose banks
the principal part of them resided. Besides the
fair Christina and Koningsmarke, the captives consisted of Counsellor Ludwig Varlett, Lob Dotterel,
a poor man named Claas Tomeson, his wife and
child, and that likely fellow Cupid, who, for some
cause or other, seemed rather to accompany them
voluntarily than by compulsion.

They shaped their course to the westward,
passing through deep forests, where the sound of
the axe had never been heard, and where the wild
animals had hitherto maintained undisturbed possession. Poor Christina was soon so worn down
with grief and fatigue, that she was incapable of
keeping up with the rest of the party, and had not
the Long Finne sometimes taken her in his arms
and carried her through the swamps, she would
have been murdered by the savages, who several
times turned back and threatened her with their
tomahawks. At the end of the first day's journey,

the luckless wife of Claas Tomeson, whose infant
was scarcely a month old, was so worn down, that
the Indians debated whether they should not put
an end to them both. Finally it was resolved upon,
and they were despatched, in spite of the shrieks
of Christina, and the agonizing cries of the husband,
who was first tied to a tree, and thus he witnessed,
without being able to make a single effort to prevent it, the fate of his helpless wife, and still more
helpless infant.

Three days more they journeyed in this manner,
Christina every day becoming more weak, and
every moment expecting to meet the fate of the
poor woman and her child. Towards the evening
of the fourth, they approached the banks of the
river on which dwelt the tribe of the Rolling
Thunder, and gave the war-whoop, which was
answered by the women, children, and old men,
that had remained at home. One of the warriors
had been previously sent to the town to inform
them of the success of the expedition, and prepare
them for a frolic. Accordingly, the party was met
about half a mile from the town, by an infuriated
rabble, armed with guns, clubs, and tomahawks,
hallooing and whooping with horrible exultation,
mixed with cries of vengeance, from the kindred
of those who had been slain, in the attack upon
Elsingburgh.

Poor Claas Tomeson was selected, on this occasion, for the object of their infernal merriment. He

was stripped, painted black with charcoal, and apprized that if he gained the door of the council-house, which was pointed out to him, he would be safe. They then gave him the start about six paces, and Claas ran for his life, followed by the yelling crew, who assailed him with every ingenuity of torture they could devise; beating him with clubs, cutting at him with their tomahawks, and sometimes putting the muzzles of their guns close to his naked skin and firing powder into it, powowing and beating their rude drums all the while. Poor Claas, although wounded and maimed in a cruel manner, animated by a last hope, exerted himself to the utmost, and at length succeeded in gaining' the door of the council-house, that sanctuary even among barbarians. He seized the door post, and at the same instant fainted under his tortures and exertions. A dispute now arose, whether he had fairly entitled himself to the condition upon which his life was to be spared, and it was with great difficulty the old men could restrain the infuriated youth from despatching him. At length it was agreed to spare the victim, at least for the present, and he was carried to a wigwam, where a doctor or conjurer was sent to attend upon him.

The first thing the doctor did, was to mumble to himself a parcel of unconnected jargon, which poor Claas as little comprehended as a civilized patient does a civilized doctor, when he describes his symptoms. He then caused a large fire to be

made, and the door to be shut, and thereupon began to cut capers and shout aloud, until he was
in 'a glorious perspiration; it being his opinion,
that whenever a patient could not take' sufficient
exercise to produce this effect upon himself, the
next best thing was for the doctor to do it for him.
So, also, if it was necessary to take medicines, or
fast, the practice of the Indian doctor was to take
the physic, and undergo the penance himself; all
which equally redounded to the benefit of the sick
man—provided the doctor was well paid.   Without that indispensable preliminary, this mode of
cure was divested of all its efficacy.   After caper-
ing himself into a fine perspiration, and swallowing
a dose of something, the doctor inquired of Claas
how he felt himself.   The poor fellow, who was
soon recovered to the use of his senses, thought it
most prudent to compliment the doctor by saying
he was much better; for he was apprehensive that
if he lost all hope of finally curing his patient, he
might cut the matter short and save his credit, by
recommending an *auto de fe;* so he professed himself marvellously benefitted.

The next day the doctor came again, cut a few
more capers, talked a little jargon, and took a drink
of strong liquor, or rum, in order to strengthen his
patient, who, as before, declared the great benefit
he received from the prescription. The third time,
the doctor brought with him his great medicine,
as he called it, which was to perfect the cure. He

began with making the most diabolical faces ima-
ginable; then he puffed, and strained, and struggled,
as if contesting with some invisible being with might
and main. Presently he ceased, crying out, at the
same time, " Mila-mila-kipokitie koasab," which, in
the learned language of the Indians, means, " give,
give me thy breeches." This being explained to
Claas, and he at the same time assured that the
success of the great medicine depended upon com-
plying with the requisitions of the doctor, he was
fain to give up his breeches. The doctor then
commenced another great contest with the invisible Maneto, whom he again tumbled on the floor
with a mighty effort, exclaiming at the same time
—" Mila-mila-capotionian," which means, " give
me thy coat." With this also poor Claas complied. Hereupon the doctor began a struggle more
desperate than the preceding, which terminated in
his crying out aloud—" Mila-mila-papakionian,"
which means, " give me thy waistcoat." Claas
parted with his red waistcoat, gorgeously bedecked
with round metal buttons, with a sore heart. In
this way the doctor gradually divested his patient
of all his valuables, and at length, looking round
to see if there was any thing left, he took from his
leathern pouch an eagle's feather, and, pulling some
of the down, blew it in the face of his patient, crying out—" *Houana ! houana !—magat ! magat !*"
" 'T is done—'t is done—he is strong, he is strong."
Then carefully gathering together the various items

of his fee, he marched with astonishing dignity and gravity out of the wigwam. In process of time honest Claas actually recovered, furnishing a pregnant example of the excellent effects resulting from the doctor's taking his own prescriptions, instead of administering them to the patient.

In the meanwhile a council had been held for the purpose of deciding the destinies of the other prisoners. Agreeably to the customs of these people, the relatives of an Indian killed in battle have the choice, either of adopting a prisoner in the room of the friend they have lost, or of putting him to death by torture. Accordingly, Christina, Koningsmarke, Counsellor Varlett, Lob Dotterel, and Claas Tomeson, the latter scarce recovered from the effects of the gauntlet he had run, were brought forth in front of the council-house, to receive their doom of death or adoption.

The mothers of three warriors slain at the attack upon Elsingburgh came forth, howling, and tearing their long black hair, like so many furies thirsting for the blood of their victims; while the young children, taught from their infancy to banquet on the tortures of their enemies, stood ready to assist, if necessary, in executing the judgment. After examining the prisoners for a few minutes, as if debating whether to yield to the suggestions of policy or vengeance, a young squaw came forward, and taking the hand of Christina, exclaimed—
" Five moons ago I lost a sister, who was carried

away by the Mohawks; thou shalt take her place, and be unto me as a sister." The old men signified their acquiescence, and the Indian girl led her white sister to her wigwam.

The wife of the chief who was slain in attempting to detain the boat, as we have heretofore stated, then stepped forth, after having for awhile contemplated the face and form of the Long Finne, and addressed the old men—"My children have lost a father, I a husband—revenge is sweet—but who will hunt for us, and supply us with food in the long winters, if I should say, let us sacrifice this white man who killed a red chief? No—let him be my slave, and hunt for me, as he did who is now gone to the land of spirits." Her choice was in like manner sanctioned by the sages, and Koningsmarke was given to the Indian widow as her husband, or slave, as she should ultimately decide.

Next came the turn of Lob Dotterel, whose bald pate excited in no small degree, the wonder of the forest kings, who had heard the story of his scalp coming off in such a miraculous manner. A grand council had been held upon his wig, but they could make nothing of it. The prevailing opinion was, that it was a great medicine, by the virtue of which Lob had escaped all damage from an operation so fatal to others, and that the high constable was a sort of wizzard, whom it would be somewhat dangerous to meddle with. After a long talk among

the old men, it was at length decided to spare him,
for the present, with a view to his instructing them
in the method of compounding this great medicine,
so important to the safety of the Indian warrior.

Counsellor Varlett and Claas Tomeson now only
remained to be adjudged, and the assemblage of
women and children began to murmur at the
thoughts of losing what is considered a high frolic
among them, in like manner as civilized women
and children delight in seeing a man hanged. The
mothers of two of the warriors slain at Elsingburgh, came forward, and clamorously demanded
their victims; a demand, which, according to the
sacred customs of the savages, must not be denied.
Their doom was accordingly pronounced, and
hailed by the dismal scalp-halloo, the signal of torture and death. The two victims were accordingly seized, stripped, and painted black, and beaten
with sticks by the women and boys. Claas Tomeson's hands were then tied behind his back with
a rope, the other end of which was fastened to a
stake about fifteen feet high, leaving sufficient
length to admit of his going round it two or three
times, and back again. A chief then addressed
the multitude, urging every topic calculated to
excite their ruling passion of revenge, and was
answered by a yell that made the vast forest ring.

Then began a scene of horror which has been
often witnessed by the dauntless spirits who marched
in the van, to the exploring and settling of this new

world, and which may, perhaps, in some measure, serve to excuse their harshness to that unhappy race, by whom their friends and brothers have so often suffered. The Indian men first approached; and fired powder into his naked skin. Then they lighted the pile, composed of sticks, one end of which was previously charred by fire laid around the post, at the distance of five or six yards. A party of these exasperated and inhuman beings, then seizing the burning brands, surrounded the wretched victim, and thrust them into his naked body. Presenting themselves on every side, which ever way he ran, he met the fiends with their burning fagots, and if he stood still, they all assailed him at once. The squaws then threw the hot ashes and burning coals upon his bare head, which, falling upon the ground, in a little while he had nothing to tread upon but a bed of fire. Claas called them cowards—women—and begged them to shoot him like men and warriors. But they only answered him with laughter, shouts, and new tortures. Claas then, in the agony of his sufferings, besought the Almighty to have compassion upon him, and permit him at once to die. "Hark!" cried the warriors; "he is a woman, he is no warrior, he cries out like a coward." Exhausted, at length, with pain and exertion, he laid himself down upon his face, gradually losing all acuteness of sensation, and apparently becoming almost insensible. But from this blessed apathy he was roused by an old

hag, who, placing some burning coals on a piece of
bark, threw them upon his back, which was now
excoriated from head to foot. ˙ The poor victim
again started upon his feet, and walked slowly
round the post, gazing with a vacant look on those
about him, and appearing hardly to know what
was going forward.   Perceiving that he was no
longer susceptible to suffering, a chief came behind
him, and buried his tomahawk in the back of his
head. ˙ He fell, and yielded his tortured spirit without a groan.   ˙

   It now came to the turn of Ludwig Varlett, who
had witnessed this scene with a degree of firmness,
peculiar to that class of people who march in the
van of civilization, in our woody progress, and
whose daily toils, dangers and exposures, gradually
render them almost insensible to fear or suffering.
Perceiving his fate to be inevitable, he resolved to
meet it like a man ; at the same time a thought
came over him, that he might possibly escape the
tortures of his poor comrade.   By means of some
little smattering of their language, which he had
acquired as a trader, he managed to make the chiefs
comprehend˙ that he was in possession of a great
medicine, so powerful, as to render those acquainted
with the secret, invulnerable to a rifle ball.   The
chiefs shook their heads, with a sort of incredulous
chuckle, and asked him if he were willing to try
the experiment in his own person.   Ludwig said
yes, and desired that five or six of them would

load their guns, while he placed himself about ten
yards distant. They did so, and the crowd stood
in breathless anxiety to witness the virtues of the
great medicine. "One—two—three—fire!" cried
he; and the next instant he lay stretched a corse.
The Indians ran up to him, and then, for the first
time, comprehending the whole affair, they became
mad with rage and disappointment. They tore
his body into pieces, scooped up his blood with
their hands, and drank it smoking hot, and finally
tossed his limbs into the flames. But the brave
Ludwig felt it not, and escaped, by his presence
of mind, the sad and lingering tortures of Indian
cruelty.

This horrible festival was concluded by a drinking match, which they were enabled to carry to
the most extravagant excess, by means of a quantity of spirits they had taken at the village of Elsingburgh. The two tribes, who had been jointly
engaged in that expedition, first separated, the one
crossing the river, in order that the remembrance
of former injuries, which is the first impulse of
intoxication in the mind of an Indian, might not
produce hostilities between the two. They then
appointed persons to secrete their arms, and maintain order during the scene which was to ensue.
The debauch then commenced, by pouring a keg
of spirits into a large kettle, and dipping it out with
wooden ladles. A scene ensued which baffles all
description. The shoutings, hallooings, whoopings,

and shrieks, of each party, were heard at intervals, during the whole night, and the morning presented the wretched bacchanals, dejected, worn out, and melancholy in the extreme. Some had their clothes torn from their backs, some were wounded, others crippled, and three dead bodies marked the bloody excesses to which barbarians are prone, when their dormant passions are excited by that most pernicious foe of savage and civilized man, strong drink.

CHAPTER III.

" I have some little smattering of Greek,
Hebrew, Chaldaic, and Egyptian,
Welsh, Irish, Dutch, and Biscayan;
Indeed, all the tongues of Europe,
Asia, and Africa, are tolerably familiar—
But in America, and the new-found world,
I very much fear there be some languages
That would go near to puzzle me."

In the meantime Christina was taken home by
the Indian girl, who was called Aouetti, which
signifies Deer Eyes, from their resemblance in
wildness and brilliancy to those of that animal.
Aouetti was considered the beauty of the village,
having, in addition to her fine eyes, a profusion of
long black hair, a pretty, round, graceful figure,
and an expression of tender seriousness in her
countenance, peculiarly interesting. The family
consisted of Aouetti's mother, an aged widow, and
the *Night Shadow*, her only son, one of the most
distinguished warriors and hunters of the tribe.
Night Shadow was upwards of six feet high, straight
as a pine, active as the deer, and brave as a lion.
He could turn his face towards any point of the
compass, and march a hundred miles through the
forest without deviating to the right or to the left;
he could follow the track of man or beast upon the
dry leaves, with the sagacious instinct of a hound;

and in hunting he disdained to pursue any but the noblest beasts of the forest. The wigwam inhabited by this family was of the better sort, having two rooms, partitioned off from each other by strips of bark.

Christina became an inmate of this simple habitation, and was treated in all respects as if she were the daughter of the same mother. Aouetti was very fond of her, and gave her the name of *Mimi,* which, in her language, signified the Turtle Dove. The mother addressed her as daughter, the young people as sister. Among the savages, all women, whatever be their rank, work, if they are capable of employment. With the exception of a few slaves, who were sometimes reserved from among their prisoners, the labours of the field and of the household, were all performed by the females. Poor Christina, whose education had little qualified her for this mode of life, made but an awkward hand at planting corn, and little Deer Eyes often laughed at her bringing up, as quite ridiculous for a woman. Christina was therefore indulged in the performance of less laborious duties, such as bringing water from the spring, just in the centre of the village ; gathering cranberries, and preparing their daily meals ; to which last she soon became adequate, as their art of cookery was extremely simple. In this manner the time passed away, heavily indeed ; but although her thoughts perpetually recurred to her home in the village of Elsingburgh, and to the kindness of her father, now dead perhaps, or if living, mourning her absence in all the anxiety of perfect ignorance whether she were living or dead ; still Christina did not sink under her misfortunes. Perhaps the secret consciousness that her lover was near, and shared her fate, contributed not a little to support her in these hours of trial.

The Long Finne, whose life, as we have before stated, was reprieved by the widow, became her slave, according to the Indian custom. For a time he was narrowly watched, and never suffered out of sight of the village. But perceiving that he preserved a cheerful countenance, and seemed by degrees to become reconciled to his situation, they gradually relaxed in their vigilance, and sometimes took him out hunting with them.

The first time this happened, the Long Finne, anxious to distinguish himself, shot so well that the savage hunters became not a little jealous ; for they are extremely tenacious of their superior skill, not only in war, but in hunting. Perceiving this to be the case, Koningsmarke designedly missed several shots, and they became highly pleased to think that his first success was merely owing to chance. By degrees, as he gained their confidence, they suffered him to go into the woods by himself to hunt, so that, if he could have endured the thought of deserting Christina, he might, in all probability, have escaped. He often debated whether it would not be better to attempt returning

to Elsingburgh with a view to apprize the Heer of
his daughter's situation, in order that measures
might be taken to ransom her; but the fear that
the savages might perhaps revenge his desertion
by the sacrifice of his fellow prisoners, deterred
him from putting this project into execution.

In the intervals of his labours, and in the evening, the Long Finne, when he had become sufficiently acquainted with the Indian language, was
amused with the conversation of an aged Indian
warrior, the father of his mistress, who resided in
the family. Ollentangi, as he was called, had been
in his day a great warrior, statesman and hunter.
But he was now nearly seventy years old, and,
being subject to rheumatism, the common malady
of the old Indians, lived a life of leisure, and passed
his time principally in smoking. Ollentangi was
considered as one of the wisest men of his tribe,
and, indeed, so far as the light of nature could carry
him, was justly entitled to the appellation of a sage.
Had his opportunities been equal, he might perhaps
have been a Solon or a Socrates. With this old
man Koningsmarke often discussed the compara-
tive excellence of the Indian religion, customs,
laws, and modes of society, contrasted with those
of civilized nations, and was frequently surprised
at the ingenuity with which he maintained the superior happiness and virtue of the savages.

It was Ollentangi's opinion, that the Great Spirit
had made the red men for the shade, and the white

men for the sunshine; the former to hunt, the latter to work.

"Your black gowns," would he say, "tell us to believe as they do, and live as they live. They say we must set about dividing our forests, putting up fences, and ploughing with horses and oxen. But who is to say what shall belong to each man, that we may put up our fences accordingly? Where are we to get oxen and horses? We have nothing but furs to pay for them, and if we leave off hunting before we have become farmers, we shall neither have furs to barter, nor meat to support us. As to our religion," continued he, "we think we can understand it, but that is more than we can say of yours. Our religion is fitted for our state of nature; it is incorporated with our habits and manners, and we must change these before we are fit to become Christians. You may in time make us bad Indians, but you will never make us good white men. Be certain that so long as we have plenty of game, we shall never become farmers, nor send our children to school, nor believe in your Gods."

"You talk of our Gods, Ollentangi," said Koningsmarke—"we acknowledge but one."

"Yes, but then vou have a Good Spirit and an Evil Spirit, and your Good Spirit is, according to your own account, not so powerful as your Bad one, who not only causes your world to be overrun with evil, but actually carries off a vast many more

people than your Good Spirit. It would seem, from
this, that he was the more powerful of the two.
Besides, your black gowns have assured me that
their Good Spirit is composed of three Good Spirits, all equal; therefore, you must have more Gods
than one."

Koningsmarke endeavoured to explain the mystery of the Trinity to Ollentangi, but without
effect. It was beyond the comprehension of the
man of nature, who continued obstinately to affirm,
that if the Great Spirit was composed of three
Great Spirits, they must have a plurality of Spirits,
and that if it was not so composed, then his doctrine could not be true. Such is the utmost extent
to which human reason can carry the man of nature.

One day Ollentangi came, and with much gravity
informed Koningsmarke that he had a great pro-
jcet in his head, for the benefit of the white men.

"Listen," said he· "That you are a miserable
race in your own country, appears certain, or you
would not have come hither to disturb us. Now
our wise men have just determined to send some
of our best conjurors out to your country to convert
your people to our belief; to teach them to hunt
the deér, and to live without cheating one another
in making bargains: what think you of this?"

"But," said Koningsmarke, "your conjurors
don't understand our language."

"Oh that is easily got over. They shall teach
your people ours," replied Ollentangi.

"Well, but the state of society is so different among us, that your conjurers could never teach us to live as you do—besides, we have so little game that if we all became hunters we should be likely to starve."

"Oh but we shall soon remedy that—we shall plant acorns, and they in time will grow into great forests of trees, and game will increase accordingly."

" Yes, but what shall we do while the trees are growing ?   We have a saying, that while the grass grows the steed starves.   It will take five thousand moons for the forest to become like these."

" Well, and how long will it take for an Indian to become a white man ?   A little tree, if let alone, will grow into a great one within a certain time. It takes longer to change men than trees.   But let us proceed ; our conjurers shall teach you, among other things, to believe in all our great medicines, to make an eagle's feather protect you from a bullet, a fish-bone ward off the lightning, and a tobacco-leaf secure you from all the dangers of the forest. They shall teach you all these things."

" But we can't be taught such things, Ollentangi; we shall not be able to comprehend, or believe that a fish-bone can be made to keep off lightning.   'T is contrary to all our experience, and, to say the truth, is too foolish for the most ignorant among us to believe.   If it is a mystery, we can't comprehend it ; if it is no mystery, 'tis no better than nonsense."

" Very well—you tell me our religion is too foolish for your wisdom, and yours is too wise for our folly. We shall teach you a little of our ignorance in these matters, that you may comprehend us ; and you shall teach us some of your wisdom, that we may comprehend you. This will be proper and neighbourly. We shall in time make men of you. I don't think your case quite desperate."

" But you will not be able to teach us ignorance, as you call it. The mind never goes backwards."

" You have just acknowledged what I want you to believe, namely, that we Indians are wiser and happier than you. I have known several white men become Indians, but I never saw an Indian turn white man. Therefore, if the human mind never goes backwards, 'tis a proof that the state of nature is better than the civilized state."

One evening Koningsmarke undertook to prove to Ollentangi, that a people who cultivated the ground had a right to take it away from those who only hunted upon it, because it was the will of the Great Spirit that the human race should increase to the greatest possible number in all parts of the world. " Now you red men pretend to occupy the whole country for a hundred miles round," said the Long Finne, " though there is but two or three hundred of you, and it is large enough, if properly cultivated, to support five hundred times as many."

" Very well," replied Ollentangi ; " you say it is the will of the Great Spirit that men should increase

and be happy. You told me the other day, I remember, that your countrymen came here to look
for land, because there were too many people and
too little land in their country. People then, by
your account, can increase too fast for their happiness. Now this never happens to us red men,
therefore we are happier than you. —Besides, you
tried to persuade me not long since, that hardly
one in a hundred of the white people were happy
when they returned to the region of souls. It is
plain, therefore, that the more people there are in
this world, the more they will want land, and the
greater will be the number of the miserable in a
future state. How is this?"

Koningsmarke undertook to explain all these
matters, but they were beyond the reach of the
old man's philosophy, although one of the most
acute Indians of the new world. Among other
things, Ollentangi laughed, a thing he very seldom
did, when Koningsmarke impeached the right of
the Indians to the forests, which they had possessed for several generations.

"Listen to me," said he—"More than twenty
thousand moons ago, a female pappoose was found,
only a month old, in the waters of a lake, lying in
a little canoe of rushes. When this pappoose grew
up, she became a great prophetess, and before she
disappeared she foretold the coming of the white
man. She performed many strange and wonderful things, such as turning night into day, and water

into dry land. As our people increased, she made this continent, which was at first but a little island; and told us to remove hither, for we lived a great many month's journey towards the rising sun. Though our people were as yet but few, we wanted room to hunt; so the squaw went to the water side, and prayed that the little island might grow bigger, for the use of her chosen people. The Great Spirit hereupon sent a great number of tortoises and muskrats, that brought mud, sand, and other things, so that, in time, the island became a great continent. In memory of this service, our tribe was divided into two parts; one of which is called the Mud Turtle, the other the Muskrat. Now, as our great grandmother made this country for our own use entirely, and on purpose that we might have plenty of room to hunt in, it is plain that you white men can have no claim upon it, but that you tell us great lies about your Great Spirit having made it for you."

At another time, Koningsmarke took occasion to treat Ollentangi's philosophy and religion with very little ceremony, affirming that it was nothing but the light of nature, which only served to lead people astray.

" Very good," replied Ollentangi—" I see every day the bears, beavers, and all other animals, pursuing their natural impulses, by which they attain to such a degree of happiness as they are capable of enjoying. The beasts that live in the woods follow, then, what you call the light of nature. Now which is the happiest, a dog that is chained up all day, whipped, and kicked into the knowledge of white men, to snarl and bite, and point with his nose, or a deer that runs wild in the forest, and pursues what you call the light of nature ?"

"I should think the deer," replied Koningsmarke.

"Very well, then," said Ollentangi; "is it not the same with men? You white men are the dogs that are chained up, and taught to bite each other; and we are the deer, that run free and wild in the woods."

Koningsmarke would then undertake to explain the distinction between man and all other animals; the former being governed by reason, the latter only by instinct, and therefore of an inferior race by nature. But Ollentangi stoutly denied that there was any difference of this kind, since, if any thing, the animals were wiser a great deal than men.

"The beaver," said he, "builds better houses than we Indians, and the fox is better lodged in winter than we. Had we been naturally as reasonable as they, we should have made our habitations under ground, at least for the cold season. You white men, it is true, build better houses than the beavers, and are better lodged than the foxes, but in attaining to this you have become a miserable, degenerate race of slaves, who do nothing but work all day long, and buy and sell every thing, from your Maker, down to the smallest article that

you possess. You see, therefore, that you have
not such good reason as you think, for running
down the light of nature, since, according to your
own account, it must have guided you at first to
all your early and fancied improvements."

Koningsmarke then strove to convey to the mind
of the poor savage, some definite idea with respect
to the distinction between reason and inspiration,
the latter of which he told him was the source of
the Christian religion. Ollentangi shook his head.

"Yes!—this is what our jugglers and conjurers
tell us. They pretend that the Great Spirit sends
his messages by them. But we don't believe it,
because it is certain that if the Great Spirit had
any messages, he would send them to the chiefs
of the tribe, and not to such contemptible fellows."

The more, in fact, that Koningsmarke conversed
with the old Indian, the more he became sensible
that it was impossible to make him comprehend
the most simple elements of our social and religious
systems. Long before the winter set in, the Long
Finne became unalterably convinced that all reli-
gions must be accommodated to the state of society,
as well as the progress of intelligence; that religion is an integral portion of both; and that the
attempt to propagate a system of faith at war with
either, must necessarily entirely fail, or, if partially
successful, be productive of great *moral evil.*

Many other discussions took place between
Ollentangi and Koningsmarke, but we have already

detailed sufficient to give some little idea of the
confined views and opinions of an Indian sage.
Besides, it is high time to return to the fair and
gentle Christina, whom, though sometimes we seem
to lose sight of, we never for a moment forget.

During the first weeks of their captivity, such
was the watchful jealousy of the savages, that Koningsmarke had no opportunity of speaking either
to Christina, or honest Lob Dotterel, who, being
neither hunter nor warrior, and having no little
boys to keep in order, sunk into a personage of
very little consequence, in his own opinion. The
miracle of his wig, however, caused him to be still
wondered at by the Indians. The Long Finne
sometimes met Christina at the spring, without
daring to talk but with his eyes. In time, however,
he was less watched, and besides occasionally
conversing, he sometimes met her in the forest
gathering cranberries. On these occasions the
desolate condition of the poor girl, thus alone in the
pathless wilderness without a friend but him, caused
the gentle Christina to forget the scar on his neck,
and the warnings of Bombie of the Frizzled Head.
A flood of tender emotions rushed on her heart at
these times, and, as the tears trickled from her
eyes, which she turned up towards him like an
infant looking to its parent for protection, she sometimes forgot to resist when he kissed them away.
The Long Finne occasionally came to the wigwam
where Christina resided, and where his visits were

not discouraged, more especially by the blue-eyed
Swede and the dark-eyed Indian maid, the latter
of whom, in a little while, learned sufficient of their
language to make herself understood on various
little occasions. She was particularly importunate
with Christina to teach her how the Indian word
kisakia, which signifies " I love," was pronounced
in her native language.

It was not long, in fact, before the gentle Christina and the Deer Eyes, with that quick-sighted
instinct common to their sex, discovered, or rather
began to suspect, that they were, or would soon
become, rivals. At least it was so with Christina ;
for the ignorance of Aouetti in the modes and customs that restrain the exhibition of certain feelings
on the part of civilized women, kept her for a long
time from knowing the state of Christina's heart.
The Indian women are as remarkable for the ten-
derness and warmth of their· affections, as the
Indian men are for their coldness and indifference.
They become suddenly and strongly attached,
especially to white men ; and, being entirely governed by the feelings of nature, do not hesitate to
take upon themselves those advances, which, among
civilized people, are the province of men alone.
The gentle and tender simplicity with which the
Indian girls of the better sort do this, is peculiarly
affecting, and takes from their advances all appearance of indelicate forwardness.

The progress of this new sentiment in the heart

of Aouetti, was indicated in the increasing languor of her eyes; her carelessness in the performance of domestic duties; her solitary walks, and her hanging about Christina's neck, kissing her, and whispering, "I love him—O how I love him!" She was accustomed, in her ramblings, to compose little extemporary songs, and hum them to wild tunes of her own fancying; one of which Christina caught, and translated, or at least imitated, in the following lines:

> My love's like the deer in the forest that skip,
> Like the cranberry's hue are his cheek and his lip;
> His spirit sits by me at night when I sleep,
> But when I awake it is gone, and I weep.
>   I love him—Oh how I love him!
>
> But his bride, his *own* bride, I never shall be,
> He loves, but he loves not, he loves not poor me;
> When he's near me I'm sad, and wish him away,
> And when he is gone, I could bless him to stay.
>   I love him—O how I *do* love him!

When Christina discovered the state of the Indian girl's heart, it did not weaken her affection for her adopted sister, or diminish her grateful recollection of the obligations which she owed to that kind-souled being. True, she did not perhaps think her a dangerous rival, or it is possible her feelings might have been somewhat different. As it was, she returned her caresses, and complied with her request to sing some of those songs that were favourites with Koningsmarke, that she too might learn them, and sing his heart away, as she expressed it in her

figurative language. Though we firmly believe
that Christina was capable of feeling and exer-
cising as much generosity as ever fell to the lot of
woman, still we will not pretend to say, that her
sympathy for the Deer Eyes, would have continued
unshaken, or survived the shock of her successful
rivalship. As it was, however, it happened that
circumstances and events occurred about this time,
that united the two maidens in one common cause
of jealousy and apprehension.

The Indians among whom our hero and heroine
were now domesticated, had long been on ill terms
with a tribe dwelling on the banks of the Ohio.
There was a world of forest between them, it is
true ; but the hunting excursions of the savages,
like the commercial pursuits of civilized men, often
made tribes who lived at a distance from each
other, neighbours and rivals. Some hundred years
before, one of the Ohio tribe had been killed by
an Indian of the Delaware, and the vengeance of
a savage never sleeps or dies. The former, not
long previous to the period to which our history
has now arrived, had sent a petticoat to the latter,
accompanied by a most insulting message, that
"they were women, and no warriors—and that
they would shortly come, and make them run into
the hollow trees like woodchucks." Such banters
were not uncommon among the savages, and this
message was considered a declaration of war.

This war message, with the reflection which it

contained, enraged the Rolling Thunder and his warriors to such a degree, that they resolved, with the approbation of the old men, to convince the Ohio Indians they were not women, by undertaking an expedition against them forthwith. Preparatory to setting out, however, they held a war dance.

This dance was accompanied by vocal and instrumental music. The latter was produced by a drum, made from a piece of hollow tree, cut off so as to leave one end closed by the wood, to hold water in the bottom. Over the other end was drawn a piece of dried skin, somewhat resembling parchment, and which, when beaten upon with a stick, produced a sound somewhat similar to a muffled drum. The party which was to go on this war expedition, collected round an aged Indian, who now began to sing, accompanying himself by striking upon the drum at regular intervals. Each of these warriors, armed either with a tomahawk, war-club, or spear, began to move forward in concert towards the west, the direction in which they were going to war. When they had advanced about fifty or sixty yards, they pointed their weapons, in a furious and threatening manner, towards their enemy, and, turning round, with a terrible shout, danced back in concert as before.

They then began the war song, which was sung by one person at a time, and consisted in relating, in a sort of recititavo, the exploits of the warrior himself, or what he was resolved to perform in the expedition.

These promises are similar to the vows of knight errantry; to shrink from their performance, is considered an indelible disgrace, and the warriors often sacrifice themselves rather than fail. At the end of the relation of every past exploit, the warrior struck a post with his tomahawk, and those who had witnessed what he related, testified to its truth by crying out—"Huh! huh!" · On the contrary, if he related any thing that was doubtful, they shook their heads, and were perfectly silent. The whole ceremony was concluded by a loud shout, and many young men who had declined going to the war, were so animated with the scene, that they immediately signified their intention to join the expedition.

They next proceeded to the ceremony of adopting Lob Dotterel, whom it was their intention to admit into a participation of the glories of the expedition; he having at length gained their confidence, by his apparent cheerfulness, and the readiness with which he accommodated himself to their habits and customs. Koningsmarke was already considered as belonging to the tribe, in virtue of the widow's choice.

The first part of this ceremony consists in pulling out all the hair, except what grows just upon the crown of the head, which is left to be dressed after the Indian fashion. As, however, Lob Dotterel had no hair upon his head, they proceeded, in lieu thereof, to infringe upon his beard, which, by this time, had grown to a considerable length. In order to proceed the more expeditiously, the person who officiated in this matter ever and anon dipped his fingers into some ashes, placed on a piece of bark, that he might take the better hold. The high constable winced at every twitch, and the tears rolled down his cheeks, to the great amusement of the spectators. This being finished, they proceeded to bore his nose and ears, into which they hung certain rich copper rings, and jewels, of unknown price, having cost them whole kingdoms.

The high constable was then handed over to three or four squaws, who led him to the river side, bidding him plunge in head-foremost. To this Lob Dotterel demurred, it being his firm belief that they intended to drown him. Upon this they laid hold of him, and, spite of his sturdy resistance, dragged him into the water, where they rubbed and scrubbed him till he had scarcely any skin remaining. He was then led to the council-house, where he was gorgeously decked with a new pair of leggins and moccasins, beaded garters, porcupine quills, hair dyed red, and finally, accommodated with a magnificent cap, made of the skin of a buffalo's head, with the horns on. Then seating him upon a bear skin, they gave him a pipe, a tomahawk, and a pouch containing the herb called killekenico, which they sometimes used instead of tobacco, and

materials for striking fire. After this, they painted
him in their best style, and with all the colours
they had in their possession. This important ceremony being concluded, an aged chief arose and
made him a long speech, the substance of which
was as follows :—

"My son—You have just had all the white
blood washed out of your body, and are now a red
chief. You are a great man, among a great nation
of warriors, and are from this day called the Jumping Sturgeon, after a mighty Mingo chief, who fell
many moons ago fighting with the Five Nations.
My son, you are now of our flesh and bone—your
heart is our heart—our hearts are your hearts—
and as you fight in our quarrels, so will we defend
and protect you as our son and brother!"

The Jumping Sturgeon was then solemnly introduced to his new kinsmen and kinswomen, and
invited to a great feast, where he ate boiled corn
with a wooden ladle, and got mortal tipsy ; which
last ceremony completed his initiation into the
Muskrat tribe. Early the next morning, the painted
warriors, accompanied by Koningsmarke and the
illustrious Jumping Sturgeon, set forth upon their
expedition to the Ohio. Koningsmarke was followed by the tears of Christina, the hopes of
Aouetti, and the encouragement of the widow,
who comforted him with the assurance, that if he
conducted himself like a brave warrior, she would,
on his return with a reasonable number of scalps,

make him sole lord of herself and her pewter work. The warriors left the village at the dawning of day, chanting their *marching song*, of which the following is a sort of translation:

To battle! to battle!
Hurrah! to battle!
Let them not see us!
Let them not hear us!
Let them not fear us!
Till they shall feel us!
    March! march!

Hush! hush! hush!
   We're on the track;
Yon fire at the bush
   Has warm'd their back!
Crawl on the earth,
Smother your breath,
Be silent as death!
    Hush! hush! hush!

They are near, they are near!
   'Tis their last, last day!
Their death song I hear;
   And now it dies away!
So shall they die;
Ere they hear our war-cry,
Low shall they lie!
    Hark! they are near!

Halt! level your guns!
   Your tomahawks lift,
Swift as the deer runs—
   Swift, swift, swift!
Spare none, not one!
Let the hot blood run;
'Tis done—'tis done!
    They are dead!

Nevermore, nevermore,
　　Shall they lift their head;
Nevermore, nevermore,
　　Shall they wake from the dead!
　　　The dead shall sleep,
　　　While the living weep.
Let them mourn, mourn, mourn;
The dead, the dead will return
　　　Nevermore, nevermore!

END OF VOL. I.

CPSIA information can be obtained at www.ICGtesting.com
Printed in the USA
BVOW06s0446231215

430809BV00020B/268/P